A CASE of MURDER by Monte Carlo

Texas General Cozy Cases

Of Mystery
Book 1

BECKI WILLIS

Cover Design by Anelia Savova (annrsdesign.com)

Editing by Elizabeth Oakes (greeneyeediting.com)

ISBN: 978-0-9987902-4-4

OTHER BOOKS BY BECKI

Forgotten Boxes
Plain Roots
Tangible Spirits
He Kills Me, He Kills Me Not
Mirrors Don't Lie Series
- The Girl from Her Mirror – Book 1
- Mirror, Mirror on Her Wall – Book 2
- Light from Her Mirror – Book 3

The Sisters, Texas Mystery Series
- Chicken Scratch – Book 1
- When the Stars Fall – Book 2
- Stipulations & Complications – Book 3
- Home Again: Starting Over – Book 4
- Genny's Ballad – Book 5
- Christmas In The Sisters – Book 6
- The Lilac Code – Book 7
- Wildflower Wedding (With a Killer Reception) – Book 8

Spirits of Texas Cozy Mystery Series
- Inn the Spirit of Legends – Book 1
- Inn the Spirit of Trickery – Book 2

CONTENTS

ACKNOWLEDGMENTS

As always, my family deserves special recognition. Roger, Winter, Jerry, Korbin, Kennedi, Kambri, Laramie, Casey, Weston, Colt, and my sweet Mother, thank you for your support and encouragement. Thank you for indulging me in my research (often incorporated into a family vacation!) and the many times I confine myself to my office or steal away on a writing retreat. Your love and support means more to me than any award or sales ranking.

For this series, I am relying on first-hand experience (and a few borrowed stories) from my daughter-in-law, Casey Willis, R.N. I always depend on my son Laramie to help spot those lingering pesky typos. Please know I love and appreciate you both!

CHAPTER ONE

"Yum," the lab tech murmured, stuffing a chip laden with spicy avocado and shrimp dip into his mouth. "This may be the winner right here." He closed his eyes to savor the explosion of flavors upon his tongue. "Perfection."

"Thanks!" Laurel Benson beamed. "I hear Ayla in Respiratory has a spinach dip to die for, so I'm anxious to see how this one compares."

It had become a tradition here at *Texas General* on Game Day, a sort of 'competition behind the competition.' While thousands of college football fans trekked to Kyle Field for their grand scale tailgating parties, each department within the hospital hosted a party at their prospective nurses' station. The Emergency Room where Laurel worked was no exception.

The hospital itself—fully embracing the time-honored tradition of Aggie football—provided health-conscious versions of fan favorites, but it was up to staff members to bring "the good stuff", the dishes oozing with cheese and calories and enough cholesterol to guarantee job security for health professionals worldwide. Creamy dips, gourmet salsas, and calorie-rich finger foods fought for space among the platters of veggie sticks and salt-free chicken wings. Decadent desserts weighed down one end of every table, tempting even the staunchest dieter with sugary fruit toppings, cream fillings, and the lure of a chocolate-induced coma. The offerings were so diverse (and so delicious) that it quickly became a competition to see who could bring the best and tastiest dish. Just one year in, and the highly anticipated contest already had a coveted trophy worth fighting for: a massive maroon and white wreath awarded to the station providing the best snacks.

"If I weren't already married," the technician claimed, eyes still closed in reverence, "I would propose marriage, right here on the spot."

"A marriage can't survive on dip alone, my friend," Laurel reminded him, reaching around his extended belly to swipe a cookie. "And if you weren't married to Glenda, I couldn't indulge in these scrumptious cookies of hers. *These*," the petite nurse proclaimed, palming a second cookie as reserve, "I could survive on."

"We may have to send the trophy home with you, Jim," a second nurse agreed, moving in behind him to fill her plate. "Glenda is like our very own secret weapon."

"Small bit of compensation," he agreed around another mouthful of dip, "for having to put up with Football Fandemonium."

It was a term they coined for the added influx of patients each Game Day, one of a half dozen or so sacred Saturdays strung between August and December when the fighting Texas A&M Aggies hosted their opponent for the week. Saturdays were naturally busy in the ER, but with tens of thousands extra footballs fans in town, the excessive celebrations, after-parties, and snarled roadways always doubled, if not tripled, their load. The bigger the school rivalry, the crazier the reason for the ER visits.

Laurel checked her watch, sinking into the rolling chair behind the desk. "It's been relatively quiet, so far," she said. The cookie made a satisfying *snap!* as she sank her teeth into it. "But I imagine the Fandemoniums will start rolling in within the hour."

The words barely cleared her lips before they heard the ambulance's wail.

"Thanks a lot," Mary Ann said, already abandoning the plate she just filled. "Look what you did."

Laurel had the grace to look apologetic, needlessly taking blame for the incoming. "Sorry. You eat. I'll take this one," she offered.

"I'm already up," Mary Ann said, motioning her to sit back down. She gave one last mournful look at her abandoned plate. "I didn't need the extra calories, anyway."

The siren's sharp trill grew louder, bleeding in ahead of the gurney as the sliding doors flew open and paramedics rushed their patient inside. "Hit and run victim!" one of the medics called over his shoulder. "Heart rate 288 with 12-lead showing V-fib, blood pressure unsteady. In and out of consciousness. Bring a crash cart, stat!"

Laurel jumped to her feet, just as a familiar chime announced the door opening from the waiting room, most likely to admit a walk-in patient. Even as she heard the rustle of fabric and voices approaching from the front, she would have abandoned her post and offered aid to the hit and run victim, had someone not beat her to it. The on-duty doctor and two more nurses rushed toward the gurney before she could round the counter.

Satisfied that the hit and run had adequate help for the moment, Laurel turned her attention to the walk-in. A thin woman followed timidly behind the medical assistant from Admissions, her steps unsteady. One glance told her that the woman was as much frightened as she was in pain.

Before returning home to the Bryan-College Station area, Laurel started her nursing career in Houston, working in one of the busiest and most acclaimed hospitals in the nation. Over six years of experience had honed Laurel's assessment skills. Almost unconsciously, she could look at a patient and make an immediate assessment call. Today was no exception.

One hundred-ten pounds soaking wet, poor posture, stooped shoulders. Possible early signs of osteoporosis. Sallow skin color, dark circles under eyes. Could be exhaustion, could be drug use. No visible signs of injury or physical trauma, so must be internal. Looks more nervous than in pain. Either way, in dire need of a hot meal and a hot shower, not necessarily in that order.

Laurel suspected the woman's hair had once been dishwater blond, but the dishwater definitely needed changing. Unkempt locks hung in disarray, streaked now with gray and a layer of grease. Her clothes weren't the tattered rags of a homeless person, but the dirt had been there long enough to set in. Making a mental note to offer a shower and change of clothes before releasing her, Laurel was thankful *Texas General* took a holistic approach to health care. The woman looked forty if she was a day, but Laurel suspected she might be several years younger. Hard living had a tendency to age women before their time, and something in her weary eyes and lined face told Laurel that life hadn't been easy for this woman.

A lanky boy in his teens trailed behind them, his eyes

enormous as they found the commotion on the other side of the corridor. Intent on the buzz of activity around the hit and run accident, he walked past the room the assistant led his mother into.

"We're right here," the assistant said brightly, redirecting the youth.

With a sheepish expression, he shuffled into the small space, but his eyes never quite left the other room.

Well aware of the drama unfolding across the hall, Laurel put as much warmth as she could into her smile when she greeted the newcomers. She knew how disconcerting it could be for other patients when they heard a crash cart mentioned.

Helping the woman settle onto the narrow bed, she noted how her small frame barely made a shadow, much less an indentation.

"My name is Laurel. Can you tell me your name and date of birth?" She read the printed information on the hospital band, waiting for verbal confirmation.

The woman's voice was scratchy and wavered with either pain or fear—Laurel would bet on the latter—but the words were clear. "L…Lily Moses. 2-25-1982." Sure enough, younger than the forty she looked.

"What brings you in today, Lily?"

Lily darted a nervous glance toward her son. "Uhm, I got a hurting in my gut and all," she said. Almost as an afterthought, she clutched at her mid-section and offered a grimace. "It hurts something powerful."

Laurel suspected something wasn't quite right with her new patient. As she fitted the blood pressure cuff around her skinny arm, winding the binding a second time to hold it in place, she asked, "How long has this pain been bothering you, Lily?"

"Oh, uhm, it started a few days ago." Another darted

look toward her son, who seemed to be more concerned with what happened across the hall than what happened here with his mother. "But it got real intense about an hour or so ago. Ain't that right, Harold?" When the boy made no reply, she called his name again sharply. "Harold!"

"Huh?" He reluctantly dragged his attention back to his mother.

She repeated her claim as Laurel clamped the oximeter onto the tip of one finger. "I said ain't that right?" There was a pointed insistence in her voice as she needled the boy with her laser-like glare.

"Oh, uh, yeah," the boy said. "'Bout an hour ago. I remember, because we were watching the game. On Channel 3."

Laurel studied the numbers on the monitor, watching as they made a valiant effort to record a stable blood pressure. She was careful to keep the look of censure off her face; even though Harold made a point to mention the channel, their local network couldn't carry the game. The boy obviously wasn't telling the truth, but why? She overtly checked for needle marks on Lily's arm as the machine failed to get a reading. When the pressure built and the cuff tightened for a second time, Laurel saw the first real look of pain cross Lily's face.

"Sorry. Sometimes it has to pump a second time. Can you describe your pain for me?" she asked, wondering if the woman was experienced in the art of hiding signs of drug abuse. She knew some addicts preferred to shoot up in the soft tissue between their toes. While she contemplated a way to talk Lily out of her shoes, the woman offered a very vague description of what she called 'terrible bad' abdominal pain.

Maybe she's just nervous. Heart rate slightly elevated and pressure 178/86. Neither necessarily indicative of severe pain or drug use, but I'll give her the benefit of doubt. The vagueness could be attributed to nerves. Emergency rooms had a tendency to do that to patients.

"Is Harold your son?" Laurel asked, offering the teen another warm smile. His attention had wandered back across the hall, where things were obviously deteriorating. The Code Blue warning still echoed in the corridor, muffled only by the sound of running feet and hurried bodies. One glance across the hall told Laurel that their patient was in dire condition.

"My oldest. Got three more at home, and all," Lily offered.

"Oh, my. Four children. What a blessing!"

Lily's quiet harrumph spoke volumes, but her son was too busy watching the other room to notice the slight.

"How old are they?" Laurel asked.

"Harold's sixteen, Danny's thirteen, Paulie's twelve, and Jill is ten."

"Is their father at home with them?" The question came out innocent sounding enough, as Laurel listened to the steady thump of the woman's heart.

"Ain't seen none of their fathers in at least five years," Lily snorted. "Don't know where two of them are, and don't care. Know exactly where Harold's old man is. State Penn in Huntsville."

"And none of them pay child support? I could put you in touch with—"

Lily interrupted her before she could finish her offer of help, doubtful though it was. "Ain't none of them got a dime to their name, much less the gumption to claim their own blood." She raised her chin a fraction and made a bold claim. "We've done just fine without 'em. Don't need the likes of none of them, coming around after all this time. Not after all the hard stuff's done been done, changing diapers and wiping snotty noses and losing a night's sleep to teethin' babies. No, ma'am, I don't need them now." She set her jaw stubbornly, but Laurel saw the slight quiver in her chin.

"Good for you, Lily," Laurel said softly. She made another mental note, this one to find a business card for an organization that specialized in helping single mothers in need. "If you'll answer a few more questions for me, I'll let you settle in and rest for a few minutes until a doctor can see you. Are you comfortable, or do you need a few more pillows?"

"Nah, I'm fine." Now Lily craned her neck, trying to see across the hall. "What's the commotion and all over yonder?"

"Car accident, I believe. Now, Lily, tell me more about this pain. Would you say it's more of a stabbing pain or a radiating pain?"

"Ain't never been stabbed before, so don't know how that would feel, and all." She nibbled on her lower lip, still watching the hustle of activity taking place across the way. "You reckon that fella's gonna make it?"

It wasn't unusual for one patient to be curious about another. Often, it helped to ease their own fears by transferring their worries to a stranger. Other times, any sign of bad news—even if applied to a stranger— was enough to send a patient into a panic attack.

No matter the reason for Lily's pointed concern, she was in no position to supply her nosy patient with answers. Strategically positioning herself in Lily's line of sight until she could tug the curtain fully shut, Laurel's answer was non-committal.

"I certainly hope so, but my concern at the moment is for you. I need you to tell me more about the reason you came in this afternoon, Lily."

A wary look moved into the woman's eyes. "Why? You don't believe me? You think I'm making all this up? I got better things to do than come down to some emergency room, I can tell you that!"

"I'm sure you do. And I'm not suggesting your pain isn't real. I just need to know more about it, so we can help you feel better."

"Maybe I oughta put on one of those gowns you offer," Lily said, cutting her eyes to her son. "Harold, step out in the hall while I change, and all."

The teen scrambled out of the chair, moving faster than Laurel had seen him do so far. No doubt, he was eager to be on the other side of the curtain, ogling the scene as it unfolded across the way.

"Do you need help changing?" Laurel asked, retrieving a folded gown from an upper cabinet and placing it on the foot of the bed.

"Nah. Never did like anyone seeing me in my skivvies," Lily said. "I'll be fine. You trot on along and see if you can help that man yonder. He looks to be in bad shape."

"Use this button here to call me if you need anything."

"Just go, and don't mind me none."

Laurel stepped out of the room, a frown crinkling her forehead. Most patients demanded prompt attention, yet Lily Moses insisted she leave her alone to tend another patient. Somehow, Laurel suspected it was hardly a magnanimous act of selflessness on her part. She couldn't help but remain skeptical.

Harold had wandered closer to the hub of activity. While he stood just far enough away not to interfere, his avid curiosity pushed the bounds of propriety. Privacy was the least of the ER team's concern as they fought to save the man's life. The curtain hung abandoned, as personnel rushed to and from his bedside.

Grabbing the plate Mary Ann had recently abandoned, Laurel took a 'round about path to meet Harold head on and herd him back in the right direction. "I thought you might enjoy a bite to eat," she said, deliberately walking between the nosy teen and the disturbing scene no one should have to witness, particularly an impressionable youth.

He craned his scrawny neck out to see around her, the irritation plain upon his face. *Dark hair, pale skin, poor muscle tone*, Laurel assessed. *Spends too much time indoors, probably on some gaming device, without getting proper exercise. Pockmarks on his face could be acne, could be drug abuse. Ripped jeans, faded black t-shirt, shaggy haircut. Among my peers, slouchy. Among his peers, borderline stylish.*

The change in fashions always made Laurel feel her age. Twenty-nine still seemed young, until little things like loud music and trendy clothes started bothering her. Still, she doubted his classmates viewed Harold Moses as a trendsetter. *Could be because he, too, needs a hot shower.*

He started to decline her offer of food, until he caught sight of the offering. The heavy-duty plate fairly sagged with the weight of the delectable game day fare piled upon it. "Well, maybe just a bite."

"Why don't you follow me to the desk, and we'll get you a drink to go with it? I can find you a chair, too, until your mom gets changed."

"Uhm, okay." He turned to follow but threw a mournful look over his shoulder. He was clearly torn. Should he watch the horrific spectacle playing out across the hall, or give in to the heady aromas wafting up from the plate?

His stomach eventually won out, and he followed Laurel without incident. She faced the chair away from the activity and offered him a soft drink, but by the time his plate was empty (mere minutes later) he had inched it slowly around and was again able to watch the comings and goings in the other room.

"Is that guy gonna make it?" he finally asked. Despite his morbid fascination with the real-life drama, the quiver in his voice belied his detachment.

Laurel knew better than to offer empty promises. "He's certainly getting the best care available," she assured the teen. "Can I get you anything else? Another piece of cake? A brownie?"

"Maybe a brownie," he agreed. He shot a look toward the abandoned table. Other than Laurel, everyone was huddled around the gurney across the hall. His eyes wandered back toward the activity. "Who hit him?"

"I don't know any of the details." She placed a brownie on a fresh plate and added a cookie for good measure. "Tell me about your mom's pain. Is this the first time she's complained about it?"

"Uh, yeah, I think so. It just came out of nowhere." He leaned back in his chair, trying to see around the technician blocking his view. His voice was distracted as he dipped his chin, then swiveled it at an angle to get a better glimpse around the interference. "Started moaning and groaning. Grabbed her stomach and said it hurt something terrible."

"Was that before or after that amazing quarterback sneak? That was quite a play, wasn't it?" Judging from her smile, there was no way to know Laurel was making it all up. She simply wanted to know if Harold had been watching the game, or if he had been wrong about the channel.

"Uh, yeah, crazy," he agreed, but without enthusiasm. He forced his eyes back to the plate she offered him. "It was after, I think. Yeah, definitely after."

Just as I suspected. He wasn't watching the game.

Aloud, she asked, "Do you know what your mom had to eat today?"

He shrugged his thin shoulders. "I guess she ate Fruit Loops, same as us."

"Did anyone else have a stomach ache?"

Harold stuffed the brownie into his mouth in one bite, speaking around the chocolate. "Didn't say so, if they did."

"Are you okay here, while I go check on my patients?"

"Yeah, yeah. I'm good." He waved her away, seemingly eager to be rid of her questions and her watchful eyes.

"Please stay here at the desk, Harold. We don't want to be a bother to doctors and nurses while they try to help other patients."

"What other patients?" he scoffed. "There's only one closed curtain, besides my mom and that guy."

"Hear that tone just now? That means someone else is coming in. So, do me a favor and stay where you are. Okay?" She was smiling, but her tone made it clear that it was not a request.

Taking his harrumph as consent, Laurel checked first on the still-dozing Mr. Chen, and then on Lily. She found the latter rummaging about in the cabinets, reinforcing her earlier suspicions of drug use.

"Lily, why aren't you in bed?"

The woman whirled around guiltily. "I, uh, was cold," she stammered. "I was lookin' for a blanket. Yeah. Lookin' for a blanket, and all."

Laurel plastered a smile onto her lips. "That's not a problem. Here's one right here at the foot of your bed. I think if you'll lie back down, you'll find the bed is much warmer on your feet than the cold tile floor."

"Maybe so," she agreed placidly, allowing Laurel to help her back onto the mattress.

"The doctor will be with you as soon as possible." Laurel spoke as she worked, making a show of opening the blanket and spreading it over her patient. "Now. Isn't that better?"

"Much warmer," Lily agreed. "Where's my boy?"

"He was having a few refreshments while you changed. Would you like for him to come back in now?"

"Yeah. And leave that curtain open, will you? I'm feeling a bit closet-phobic with it pulled shut, and all."

It was a flimsy excuse, butchered word and all. Laurel compromised by pulling the curtain half-way open.

To Lily's dismay, it was the wrong side to see into the other room.

CHAPTER TWO

"Harold, your mom is ready for you now," Laurel informed the teen in the hallway.

True to his word (if a grunted harrumph was considered a promise), he was still seated, but the chair was at least six feet further out into the corridor, allowing for an unobstructed view of the room across the hall.

"I'll just finish my drink," he said.

"If you don't mind, I'll have to ask you to step inside with your mom. There's another chime, so yet another patient is coming in." The Fandemonium was right on schedule now, bringing in one patient after another. She wanted to know Harold was inside the room before she checked on the newcomer.

"They took some chick in that room," he offered, pointing to the first room. "Looked like a cut on her arm."

Laurel gave the boy a firm look. "Please remember to respect the privacy of other patients, or I'm afraid I'll have to ask you to return to the waiting room."

"Hey, it's cool." The boy stood, lifting his palms into

the air. He offered a sheepish smile, but his eyes slid off to the side. He was obviously more concerned about losing access to events across the hall than he was with keeping his mother company. His foot hit the leg of the chair as he turned, but he made no offer to return it to the desk, or to pick up his abandoned plate.

Irritated by his rude behavior and his nosiness, Laurel opened her mouth to ask him to leave. She had taken pity on the teen and his mother, sensing their nervousness and thinking she was doing them a favor by keeping them together, but she had little tolerance for insolence. Before she could say a word, a woman stormed down the hallway, her voice frantic.

"Where is he? Where is my husband? What have you done with him?"

Shifting her priorities, Laurel gave Harold the briefest of glances to assure he was back where he belonged, before turning her attention to the woman barreling down the corridor.

"May I help you, ma'am?"

"You can tell me where my Raul is!" she retorted, jerking open the first curtain and peering inside. A stifled cry of alarm greeted her. Undaunted, the woman moved along and swept aside the next curtain, where Mr. Chen still softly snored.

"Ma'am!" The tone of Laurel's voice was sharp enough to give the woman pause. "Please! Control yourself."

"My Raul!" the woman lamented. "Where is he?"

Fifty-five, too old and too heavy to be wearing neon pink leggings, Laurel quickly assessed. *Not sure I can take her if she turns confrontational. More table muscle than arm muscle, but all those diamonds could put an eye out. May need a hefty dose of Valium on standby if the husband doesn't pull through.*

Hurrying toward her, Laurel mentally calculated the effective dose needed for a woman of her heft.

Laurel reached for the woman's arm, intending to pull her aside to stop her tirade down the hall, but had her hand shaken away. "They say a car hit him! Drove right over him and fled like a coward!"

Harold stood frozen in his mother's half-opened room, his face void of all color as the hysterical woman's frantic march reached their room. The teen stood aside and stared at her, mouth hung open, as she swept her gaze across the space. Lily hovered there on the bed, her face as pale as her son's, the blanket drawn up to her neck. Something akin to fear flickered in Lily's eyes before she quickly looked away.

I can't allow this woman to terrorize our patients. Behemoth or not, this has to stop! Laurel stiffened her spine and took the woman's arm in a firm grip, refusing to turn loose this time. "Ma'am, I must insist that you come with me. Can you tell me your name?"

"Esmeralda Gonzales. You have my husband, Raul. Why won't you lead me to him?" The woman rounded on Laurel, staring down at her in challenge.

There were times, like now, when Laurel's petite frame put her at a disadvantage. At five four, she was several inches shorter than Mrs. Gonzales, who was tall even without the spiked heels. Laurel suspected she was also about a hundred and thirty pounds lighter than the woman, give or take ten pounds. She refused to let that intimidate her, however. Worried or not, the wife had no right barging into *her* ER and frightening *her* patients! Laurel had seen the look that crossed Lily's face. Noted the way Harold had shrunk back in fear, his face slack and his eyes wide. She had taken an oath to protect her patients, and protect them she would! Even against whirlwind wifezillas like Esmeralda Gonzales.

"We had a patient brought in by ambulance about fifteen minutes ago. Please wait here, while I check our records and see—"

For the first time, Esmeralda noticed the activity spilling out from the other room. She took off at a lope, her heels making a racket on the tiled floor as she reached out her arms and wailed in dramatic fashion, "I'm coming, Raul! Hang on, baby, Mama's on her way!"

Laurel had to jog to keep up with her, trying, in fact, to beat her across the hall. Again, her shorter legs were at a distinct disadvantage as the other woman's long legs gobbled up the distance. Laurel skidded to a stop just behind her, as Esmeralda Gonzales burst her way through the personnel gathered around the gurney.

"Raul! My God, Raul, wake up! Is he dead? He's dead, isn't he? I insist you tell me what's happening, right this instant!"

Laurel lifted her hands helplessly, mouthing an apology to the doctor at the brunt of the wife's demands. With a simple acknowledgment to Laurel, Dr. Baek gave his full attention to the woman still spewing one question after another. Her words were now coming out in a fast, jumbled mix of English and Spanish. Thankful to turn the wife over to the attending team, Laurel murmured an inquiry to the nurse rooted out into the hallway.

"What's the story?"

"Hit and run," Danni Barrington said, keeping her voice low. "He's in bad shape, but I think we have him semi-stabilized for the moment."

"Was he in a car, or on foot?"

Laurel's stomach sank when she heard the reply. "On foot. If he pulls through, he'll likely lose one or both legs. The bones are crushed beyond repair."

"How tragic."

The tone sounded again, alerting the arrival of another walk-in patient. "Do you need help?" Danni offered.

Laurel tipped her head to one side, the loose curls brushing the side of her face. "Thanks, but I think I hear sirens, too. Sounds like we've got another ambulance on the way."

Danni blew out a weary sigh. "Definitely Game Day."

Picking up the pace, Laurel headed for the first room. She hated making patients wait, but sometimes, like now, it couldn't be helped.

Halfway there, she saw the medical assistant leading the latest patient around the corner. Two men staggered behind her, seemingly holding the other up. Both were huge men, tall and muscled, and could pass for football players themselves, especially dressed in maroon and white jerseys as they were. At first glance, she wondered which one was the patient and which was the support, until she saw a trickle of blood making its way down one of the men's faces.

Three hundred pounds, easy. Excellent physical condition. Possible pro ball player. Could easily bench press me without breaking a sweat, despite being obviously inebriated. Laceration near the periorbital area. Frontal sinus fracture could be a concern. Doesn't seem to be in pain, but wait until the party afterglow wears off. A tiny smile tickled the corners of her mouth. *Appears to have a Siamese twin, except that his twin is white and bald, as opposed to black and sporting dread locks.*

She spoke as she passed, promising to be right with them. The injured man offered her a lazy, drunken grin.

"Where ya goin', nurse? I neeeed you," he protested.

Laurel spoke over her shoulder. "Bridgett will get you

settled in, and I'll be with you shortly."

She stepped into Room 1, where a young woman held a bandage onto her bleeding arm.

Early twenties, possibly a college student. Looks frightened, so probably first time in ER without momma. Doesn't appear to be a bleeder. Moderate pain, above-average fear.

"Oh, my, it looks like you have a nasty cut. I'm Laurel, and I'm sorry it took me so long to get here." She gave the young woman a warm smile as she gloved up. Moving close to the bedside, she wanted to assure the girl with her presence before proceeding. "What's your name, sweetheart?"

"C...Carly. Carly Acosta."

"Do you mind if I take a look at your arm?" When the girl thrust her arm out for inspection, Laurel carefully pulled the bandage away. A bit of blood still seeped from the gash, which looked about an inch and a half long. "Oh, my. How did you acquire this?"

"It was stupid, really. We—a big group of us in the dorm—were watching the game on TV, and I was about to slice another stick of summer sausage. We made a touchdown, everyone cheered, someone spilled a drink, someone bumped into me, somehow I got cut. Stupid, but it happened."

"Let's get this cleaned up really well and we'll see what we have. I think it might need a couple of stitches, but luckily for you—" she paused for effect, using exaggerated flair to make the bold claim "—*I* am an excellent seamstress." She felt the girl's arm relax, just as she hoped, as a timid smile stole across her pale face.

As Laurel gathered the supplies she would need to clean the wound, she tried to ease the girl's fears with casual conversation. She learned the girl was an engineering major from Odessa. Even though she was now a sophomore at the University, being almost seven hours from home, she still battled a severe case of homesickness. And yes, this was her first visit to the ER without one of her parents present.

Sometime around the antiseptic, Carly felt comfortable enough to ask a question of her own. "If you don't mind me asking, why did Mrs. Gonzales open the curtain earlier? She looked like she was searching for something."

Laurel looked up in surprise. "You know her?"

"Of course. She owns *Mama G's Taqueria.* They have *the best* fish tacos you can imagine. They will blow your mind."

"I don't believe I've ever eaten there. Where are they located?"

"They have three locations, but we always eat at the one on Holleman. I hear her husband runs the one in downtown Bryan, and it's really good, too. The new one is out on Rock Prairie."

Three locations. Could explain all the diamonds.

"I hear they're going through a nasty divorce, and that the husband is trying to get control of the Rock Prairie restaurant," Carly continued.

Hmm. She certainly seemed distraught earlier. Maybe this accident will bring them closer and make them remember why they got married in the first place, Laurel thought to herself.

To her patient, she said, "I'm sorry if she frightened you. I have no idea how she got back here, or why she thought it was appropriate to look into each room. I do apologize for that."

"It's okay. I just hope nothing is wrong?"

Laurel offered a noncommittal smile. "We directed her to the right place." With no further explanation, she began cleaning up her trash. "I'm going to let this air out for a bit. It will probably continue to bleed a little, so dab it with this gauze as needed. There's plenty, so don't be afraid to get a fresh piece. If it starts to bleed more than this, be sure and hit the call button." She adjusted covers and made certain everything was within the girl's reach. "Can I get you anything else? Maybe some ice water? It may be a few minutes before the doctor can come in and take a look."

"I'm good for now. Thanks."

"Sure. Buzz if you need me."

Stepping into the hall, she encountered Bridgett coming from the Fandemonium's room. The medical assistant hesitated for only a moment before rushing into an apology. "I'm really sorry about earlier. That woman just pushed her way past me. I didn't even have time to warn you. I normally like to walk the spouses back, but she was having none of that. She was like a bulldozer, just plowing her way through."

Laurel placed a comforting hand on the other woman's arm. "I understand. Don't take it too personally. Let's just try to do better in the future, okay? We can't have that scene repeating itself."

"No, ma'am. I'll make sure that it doesn't. Again, I'm really sorry."

"Thanks, Bridgett. How's it looking out there?"

"Filling up, as expected."

Drawing in a deep breath of encouragement, Laurel pasted a smile on her face as she entered the next room and donned fresh exam gloves.

Wow. The fumes are strong enough in here to get drunk on. That must have been some tailgate party!

"Hello, again. I'm Laurel. And let me guess. *You* are the patient." She pointed to the black man sitting in the chair, while his white friend sprawled on the bed.

"Got a little scratch on my head is all," he said. He wore the same goofy grin as before.

"I have an idea. Let's have you switch places with your friend, so I can take a look. What's your name?"

"They call me Knuckles."

His friend roused from the bed, glaring at him in contempt. "That's what they call *me*, you dimwit! They call you Block."

The huge man actually giggled. "Oh, yeah. They do."

Rolling her eyes, Laurel knew these two would be a handful. She used a no-nonsense voice to bark out instructions. "Knuckles, off the bed. Block, give him your chair."

Block swayed precariously as he stood. For one awful moment, Laurel thought he might fall forward and crush her beneath him. With one hand on the wall, the big man steadied himself until he regained his balance. Laurel stood back while the two men moved about the room, crowding the space with their bulk. It took far longer than it should have for the patient to settle upon the bed and swing his tree-sized legs onto the mattress.

"Made it!" he cried in triumph, still grinning.

"Yes, you did." In spite of herself, Laurel smiled. His delight was genuine, even if ridiculous. "Can you tell me your real name and your birthday?"

"Harold Bevans."

Two Harolds in one day. What are the odds? Laurel mused. She was still waiting for his second answer, which required considerable thought. After two close guesses, he finally got his birthday correct, so she presented him with another question.

"So what happened? What brings you in today?"

For the first time, his silly grin faltered. A sheepish look replaced it as he admitted, "I fell off a barstool."

On a scale of one to ten of *Crazy Reasons to Visit the ER*, Laurel gave it a five. Working in a college town full of bars and drinking establishments, she had heard the complaint before.

"The old spinning barstool, huh? And I guess you hit the floor a little too hard with your head?"

"Nah. Got this on the way down." He pointed somewhere in the general vicinity of his head, even though his actual aim pinned the pillow behind him. "The chick beside me had some wicked chains and a big, shiny buckle on her boots. Musta hit one of them when I fell."

Knuckles hooted with laughter. "It wasn't her *boots* you had your face buried in, bro!"

"Wouldn't have bothered for such a little scratch," the big man continued, the silly grin resurfacing, "but her scream scared the bartender."

"Scared him worse when she fainted from the sight of your blood," his buddy snickered.

"He says you gotta sign a release form, sayin' I ain't really hurt and I can't sue him for neggi—negli—negligee." The butchered word ended on a hiccup.

"Negligence," Laurel supplied. "And that isn't up to me, my friend. Can you turn your head for me, so I can get this cut cleaned up? By the way, it may sting just a little."

Judging from the big man's toe-curling scream, it did just that.

CHAPTER THREE

Laurel was still chuckling as she pulled off her exam gloves.

You would think I poured undiluted alcohol into his wound. What's that they say? The bigger the man, the bigger the baby? On the bright side, he did sober up rather quickly.

His friend, however, was another matter. He was still asking for Laurel's number as she pulled back the curtain and stepped into the hall. She was eager to get a breath of fresh air.

Too much testosterone and alcohol for these delicate lungs!

Laurel promptly collided with a warm, solid form. Surprise warred with embarrassment, and she jerked her head up to see the object of her discomfort.

Great! Even more testosterone! A sinking feeling settled somewhere near the bottom of her stomach, where something else had already started to swirl. That swirl meant nothing but trouble. *This time, testosterone in a* very *handsome package. Six one, slender build, excellent muscle tone. Healthy skin, good teeth, gorgeous brown eyes. Can't imagine what* he*'s doing in the ER. Every inch a healthy, virile male.* A silly adaptation to an old memory came to mind. *Run, girl, run,* *fast as you can. Gotta outrun the testosterone man.*

"I'm so sorry. My fault," she said gracefully, trying to pull back. Never mind that her traitorous body was quite content, smack dab against his muscled chest.

"No, it was mine. I wasn't watching for cross traffic."

It was a strange thing to say, until she made a belated observation. *Blond hair clipped short and neat. Khaki pants, starched blue shirt. No tie but wearing a suit jacket. No-nonsense set to his jaw. Stern look on his face, no smile whatsoever. Definitely law enforcement. Either a Texas Ranger or a detective. I repeat. Run, girl, run.*

"No problem." Laurel forced a smile. "After you, Officer."

His spiked brows spoke volumes.

"You have the look," she explained.

"Very observant." He thrust out a hand. "Detective Cade Resnick, College Station Police Force."

She tucked her small hand into his, bracing for the zing of electricity she knew would come. She wasn't disappointed. "ER Charge Nurse Laurel Benson, *Texas General Hospital.*"

"In that case, you may be just the woman I'm looking for."

From anyone else, the words might have sounded like a come-on. The brisk tone in Detective Cade Resnick's voice made it anything but that.

Before Laurel could answer, Knuckles poked his bald head from between the crease in the curtains. "Don't bother, officer," he advised. "She'll break your heart. She left mine in pieces, not to mention what she did to my buddy. He's almost in tears."

Laurel rolled her eyes at the dramatic claim, delivered amid a haze of alcoholic fumes. "That's because he sobered up and could feel the full sting of the antiseptic."

"See? See? She's coooold," Knuckles complained.

"In that case, Nurse Benson," the detective replied smoothly, "could you warm your friend up with a nice cup of strong, black coffee? If that doesn't work, I may have a pair of handcuffs that will do the trick."

Instead of being threatened, Knuckles was amused. A broad grin, not unlike his friend's formerly goofy smile, stretched across his face. "You may have found your match, little lady. And with that, I graciously bow out."

Laurel winced when she heard the racket on the other side of the curtain. *Not sure about the gracious part.* She suspected he tripped over the chair—or perhaps his own big feet—but a stern shake of the detective's head kept her from checking on him.

"He'll be fine," he said with calm certainty. "If you can tell me where to find a recent hit and run victim brought in by ambulance, I'll let you get to making that coffee."

Laurel immediately bristled. *Is he being condescending? Assuming my skills only extend as far as making coffee?*

Another clatter from the other side of the curtain reminded Laurel that the detective was right. Knuckles needed help sobering up, and now wasn't the time for her pride to rear its ugly head. The hospital couldn't release Block into his care if both men were under the influence.

"I believe you're referring to the patient in Room 6. First room on the left hall, where all the... oh. Looks like they've already moved him. They must have taken him up to surgery, second floor."

"You weren't the nurse in attendance?"

"No, that would be Nurses Beene, De Marco, and Barrington." She looked around to catch a glimpse of someone who had helped with Raul Gonzales. Even Esmeralda Gonzales and the band of personnel had vanished while she cared for the other patients. More time must have passed than she thought. "Dr. Baek was the attending physician," she offered, "but I believe he's in with another patient at the moment."

"I'll wait, if you don't mind."

"Of course not. In fact, we have refreshments, if you'd care to have a bite while you wait." She flashed a smile, this one sincere. "Game Day tradition," she explained.

A curt nod acknowledged the invitation. "I saw the table in the waiting room. I remember now that *Texas General* has a reputation for being a bit unorthodox."

He made it sound like a bad thing. Instead of bristling, Laurel turned up the wattage of her smile and quoted the hospital's tag line. "Unique health care. For Texans, by Texans." Dropping her voice to a conspiratorial level, she confided, "I've seen what they offer out there. This is where we keep the good stuff."

The detective instinctively leaned in when she dropped her voice. The woodsy scent of his cologne was a welcome change to *Eau du Coors,* but it wreaked havoc on her breathing just the same. She struggled to keep her voice light as she continued, "Help yourself to the microwave in the break room, right through there, if anything needs warming up. If you'll excuse me, I need to check on my next patient."

Busy readying Mr. Chen for a move upstairs, Laurel had no way of knowing that the detective had missed lunch that day and found the Game Day smorgasbord particularly tempting. She didn't know that he filled his plate and carried it to the break room for a quick zap in the microwave.

And she certainly didn't know that, once inside the privacy of the secluded room, the no-nonsense detective indulged in a huge smile, thoroughly amused by the refreshing Nurse Benson.

Two Fandemoniums later, Laurel had all but forgotten about the handsome detective.

That was the story she was going with, anyway. Even with herself. Who had time to fantasize about tall, gorgeous men who blew the testosterone meter completely off the charts? He hinted that he didn't approve of *Texas General's* innovative approach to holistic health care, and that he thought her best suited for kitchen duty. She wouldn't waste valuable brain cells on cave-man mentality, even if it belonged to the sexiest man she had seen in some time. She had patients to care for and work to do. *Run, run,* she would.

She proved her seamstress skills to Carly Acosta and sent Harold 'Block' Bevans home with a spiffy new bandage and a semi-sober, broken-hearted friend. (Personally, she thought her rebuff hurt Knuckles' egotistical pride, more than it did his feelings.) With Mr. Chen checked into a room upstairs and Lily Moses still complaining of pain that didn't show up on X-rays or toxicology reports, Laurel checked an expectant mother for false labor pains and reassured an armchair coach that his chest pains and severe indigestion were most likely a result of eating too many hot wings during a nail-biting win for the Aggies, rather than the heart attack he suspected. By the time she made it back to the desk for the first break in over three hours, she was exhausted.

"Another Game Day lives up to the hype," she moaned, sinking into the first chair she found. The cushions, though thin, welcomed her weary bones as graciously as the finest feather bed.

"Thirty more minutes," Danni grinned. "Then we hand over all the fun to the night shift. That's when the real doozies come out, anyway. Plenty of time to get good and drunk and celebrate another Aggie win in style."

"I see we have reason to celebrate, as well." With a smile, she nodded to the huge wreath on the break room door.

"They said your spicy shrimp dip tipped the scales."

"Cool. What's the word on Raul Gonzales?"

"He pulled through surgery, but it's still touch and go."

Laurel winced in empathy. "His legs?"

Danni shook her head in regret. "Had to take them both."

"That's horrible! Did they find who hit him?"

"No, but there was a really hot detective here, asking a ton of questions."

"Oh, I ran into him," Laurel assured her friend. "Literally."

The monitors went off on the panel, alerting them to a problem in Room 5. "That's Lily Moses' room," Laurel said. "*Again.* This is the third time we've gotten an alarm, but when I get in there, she looks perfectly fine. No signs of distress, no matter what the monitors say."

"Maybe it's a faulty machine. What alarms?"

"First, it was the blood pressure cuff. Her pressure dropped drastically, but when I took it manually, it was fine. I changed the machine. Right after that, it was her heart monitor. Sky high, erratic beat. I get in there, she looks perfectly calm and relaxed. Now it's her blood pressure again, all wonky. I don't know what is going on with her. Nothing shows up on any tests, but she insists she's in tremendous pain."

"Want me to go this time?"

Laurel pushed out of the chair with a sigh. "No, I've got it. Thanks, though. On the other hand, if you'd like to help with my charting…" She offered her best smile, hoping her co-worker would take pity on her.

As she opened the curtain to Lily's room, Harold shuffled away from the bed and back to his chair, tugging on the arm of his t-shirt. The boy looked as tired and weary as she felt.

"Lily? Are you feeling alright?" she asked in concern.

"Uhm, I still got the hurting, and all. And—And I threw up again."

The news surprised Laurel. "Again? I didn't know you *had* thrown up."

"Oh, yeah, yeah. Several times before we left the house. Once after we got here and all, and again now."

"This is the first you've mentioned it, Lily." The reprimand was in her tone. "Why didn't you tell the doctor you were having trouble keeping things down?"

"I—I guess it slipped my mind." Her eyes slid away almost guiltily, making Laurel wonder once again if she were making up some of her symptoms.

"You should have called me. I would have helped."

"That's okay. Harold helped me clean it up and all."

Laurel turned her gaze to the boy. "How did you dispose of the vomit, Harold?"

Looking squeamish and slightly green at the mere mention of the word, the boy made a grimace and pointed toward the restroom. "Flushed it down the toilet, quick as I could."

"Hmm. If it happens again, please call me. I'd like to see the volume and content."

The teen's lip curled in repulsion. "Whatever," he said, a shimmy moving through his thin shoulders. The worn-out collar of his t-shirt sagged with the motion, offering a glimpse of an angry red mark near his collarbone. Laurel noticed another red mark near the bottom of his sleeve. She wondered if the boy had been in a recent fight.

"I know you must be exhausted, Harold. Have you had a chance to move around and get a bit of fresh air?"

"A little."

"Did you find the vending machines?"

His shrug made her wonder if he had money to put in them, even if he found them.

"I think we have a few cookies and drinks left," she offered. "I'll bring you some in before I go off shift."

"What about me?" Lily wanted to know. "Don't I get nothing to eat?"

"Not if you're sick at your stomach, I'm afraid. Actually, I came in because your blood pressure alarm went off again. Does your cuff feel all right?" Laurel checked the fittings, finding it was on upside down. She frowned her disapproval. "Did you take this off, Lily?"

The woman's eyes darted to her son. "Uh, yeah. When I upchucked. Didn't want vomit to get on it and all. Harold musta put it on wrong."

"That's what we're here for, Lily. To help you with things like that. Don't be bashful about pressing that button."

"Sorry, nurse. I'll try to remember."

"Is there anyone we need to call, to check on your other children? Someone's with them, right?"

"Oh, sure, sure. My neighbor keeps an eye on them

for me. We single moms have to stick together, and all."

"I'm sure you'll be back at home with them shortly."

Instead of looking relieved, Lily looked alarmed. "You mean… they ain't keeping me overnight?"

"That's up to the doctor, but so far, all of your tests have come back negative. I'd say there's a very good chance you'll be sleeping in your own bed tonight." Laurel offered a warm smile, hoping to reassure the woman. "Doesn't that sound nice?"

"Uhm, yeah. Swell." Her lie was so obvious, Laurel's brows drew together in concern.

"Lily, is there some reason you don't want to go home? Do you not feel safe there?"

"Of course I feel safe!" the other woman huffed. She pulled the covers up around her in a defensive manner. "Why on earth wouldn't I?"

"I don't know. But if there is a reason, you can talk to me, you know." Laurel's voice was soft and full of compassion. "I'll do my best to help you. *And* your children."

"I just want to find out what's wrong with me, and what this hurtin' is about," she insisted. "That's the only reason I want to stay tonight. To find out what's wrong with me."

"I'll update the doctor on this latest news of vomiting and see what he has to say. If it happens again, please press the buzzer. Okay?"

"Yeah, sure."

"I'll stop back in one last time before I leave," she promised. "Harold, if you'll come with me, I'll get you those cookies."

Someone had cleared away the refreshment table, but Laurel rummaged around in the refrigerator until she came out with half a sandwich, a small container of dip, and two soft drinks. She grabbed her secret stash of Glenda's cookies and brought it out to give to Harold.

To her surprise, Detective Resnick was back at the desk, scribbling in a small notebook.

"Hello again, detective. Harold, here you go. These should tide you over until you know what's happening with your mom. If she stays overnight, you have a ride home, right?"

"Got our car," he mumbled, avoiding looking at the detective. Laurel wondered if he had a valid driver's license or if, like most teens, he was naturally nervous around law enforcement. He turned away without thanking her, making her almost regret her decision to give up her coveted cookies.

"Who's the kid?" the detective asked as Harold shuffled away.

"His mom came in about the same time as Mr. Gonzales, complaining of a stomachache. Poor kid's been here all afternoon. If he's like most teenagers, I know he's starving, even though I made him a plate earlier."

"You've got teens at home?" he asked, his eyes flickering down to his notebook. Along the way, they may have skittered over to her ring finger.

"Brothers," she grinned, sinking back into her chair. "I remember the hunger years, all too well."

Instead of sharing something about himself, the detective offered as an aside, "I saw him up on the second floor, wandering around the waiting room where the Gonzales family is gathered."

Laurel's tender heart went out to the teen. "Like I said, they came in about the same time as Mr. Gonzales, and he saw most of the drama unfold. I think he was pretty shaken up. Like many people, he seemed to have a morbid fascination with what was happening, but I think it affected him more than he's letting on."

"Could be," Detective Resnick said, but he didn't sound convinced. "I have a few more questions I'd like to ask, if you don't mind."

"Sure, but I doubt I can be of much help. As I said, Danni helped attend. I wasn't part of the care team."

Danni beamed up at the handsome detective, obviously more than willing to cooperate.

Not for the first time, Laurel envied her friend's voluptuously full figure and easy, dimpled smile. While both women were about the same petite height and sported a head full of short, natural curls, that was where the similarities ended. Danni's corkscrew ringlets were a fun, vibrant rust color and danced around her face with a life of their own. Laurel's looser curls were so dark they were almost black. Not even thirty years old yet, and a few wiry gray strands were already weaving their way amid the dark silk. Danni was full of curves and knew how to wear clothes that enhanced her best features. Laurel was slim and straight, but in all the wrong places.

She moved on to her chair, preparing herself for the inevitable. Men always gravitated toward Danni. She had the personality to go with the looks.

Sometimes, Laurel feared the same could be said for her. She fell flat in so many ways.

"I've already taken Miss Barrington's statement. I'd like to talk with you, if you can spare a few moments."

Clearly surprised, Laurel blinked up at him. "Okay."

If the detective expected her to stand and join him for a private conversation, he underestimated her exhaustion. He looked slightly irritated when she continued to sit there, waiting for the questions to begin. The muscles tightened around his mouth, but he flipped his notepad to a new page and began.

"I understand you were the first to speak with Mrs. Gonzales."

"Yes, that's right. According to Bridgett in registration, she more or less pushed her way in and stormed down the hall, searching for her husband."

"Can you describe to me what happened?"

Laurel had been too busy to give the incident more thought, but now that she had time to reflect on it, it made her angry all over again. She felt the huff building within her.

"She stopped at every single room, jerking open the curtains and peering inside. I heard one patient yelp in fear. I saw another patient shrink back in shock, obviously frightened. By that time, I had reached her and tried to pull her aside, but she knocked my hand away."

An odd light touched the detective eyes. "Are you saying Mrs. Gonzales assaulted you?"

"What? No, of course not! The woman was obviously distraught. She didn't mean me any harm, but she was frightening my patients. I had to stop her."

By now, the light had clearly turned to amusement. "And did you?"

He's laughing at me? He's obviously wondering how little ol' me stopped big ol' her!

"Did I what?" she fairly snapped. She refused to make it easy for him, not if he was going to make fun of her.

"Stop her."

"She didn't open any more curtains," Laurel said, a prim expression upon her lips. She neglected to point out that there had been no more along that hallway. "I was attempting to calm her down and reason with her when she spotted her husband's room and all the personnel gathered there."

"And then what?"

A smile itched at her lips as she recalled the way Esmeralda had loped off like a horse, her spiked heels clattering like horseshoes upon the tiled floor. She had been quite the spectacle, a woman of her bulk in neon pink leotards, a leopard skin top, and arms flailing above her head, diamonds catching and sparkling in the light. Stifling a giggle, Laurel tried her best to give the grave situation the seriousness it deserved.

"She ran all the way to his room," she finished simply.

"And you were…?" He left the question open-ended.

Laurel offered a rueful smile. "Trying to catch up. Quite frankly, her legs were longer than mine."

"And once she reached the room? Do you recall anything she said?"

"She demanded that her husband wake up. She thought he was dead. She had a steady barrage of questions after that, but I thought the doctor and the attending team were better suited to answer them, so I left and came back to my side of the hall."

"Your side?"

"We generally divide the workload by hallways. Since we had two serious patients on the left hall, I had the right hall primarily on my own today."

He asked a few more questions, following up with a request for her business card. "I may have more questions in the future."

"Certainly," she agreed. She pulled out a second card so that she could give it to Lily. "Why all the questions about Mrs. Gonzales?"

"Just being thorough." Cade Resnick slipped a business card from his pocket with long, nimble fingers and slid it across the desk. "And here's my card, in case you think of something else you may have forgotten."

"Absolutely, although I doubt I have anything to add."

"Just in case," he reiterated. His brown eyes held hers for the briefest of moments, before he swept his gaze across the space to include Danni. "Ladies, I appreciate your cooperation. Again, if you think of anything you may have forgotten, please don't hesitate to call. Have a good evening."

"You too, Detective," Danni called in a singsong voice, the giggle just below the surface.

"Have a nice evening," Laurel added.

The man had barely turned his back before Danni broke out in silent laughter and whispered, "I'm green with envy! Detective Hot Stuff just asked for your number!"

"He did not!" Laurel hissed, just a little too loud. She lowered her voice and repeated, "He did not. He simply wanted to know how to get in touch with me."

"Exactly! He didn't ask for *my* card."

"Well, I am Charge Nurse," she reasoned. "It's probably a chain of command thing."

"Sure it is. I think he's just got the hots for you!" Danni clapped her hands together in glee, enjoying teasing her blushing friend. "Detective Hot Stuff has the hots for Laurel!"

"Shh! Would you keep your voice down?" she hissed. "He's going to hear you!"

They both stared after the man, judging if he was within hearing range. When he stopped and turned back toward them, Laurel thought she might go into cardiac arrest.

"And by the way. My congratulations to whoever made the spicy shrimp dip with avocado. It was superb."

"Laurel!" Danni said, hopping up from her chair with

an excited clatter. "Laurel made it!"

"Good job, Laurel."

Laurel stared after his retreating back, uncertain of what shocked her the most. For all his no-nonsense by-the-book protocol, his informal use of her first name came as quite a surprise.

On top of that, the man had actually smiled at her.

And Detective Hot Stuff has a very attractive smile, she acknowledged.

CHAPTER FOUR

By the time Laurel got home, the muscles in her legs were on fire. Her feet hurt, her back ached, and she could catalog half a dozen places in between making similar complaints. She went directly to the bath and drew up a tub of hot water so she could soak away her aches and pains.

The old claw-foot bathtub was one of the things she loved most about her home. Unlike the new builds in the trendier areas of town, she lived in a remodeled craftsman located in an established old neighborhood. The houses sat back further from the sidewalks, the trees were larger and more mature, and colorful flowerbeds danced around the covered porches. With more older couples living there than college students, it was a quiet street that suited her well.

Her friends couldn't understand why she chose to live *here*, instead of in one of the more modern apartments that were springing up all over the twin cities. If it was a house she craved, duplexes lined street after street in neighborhoods much closer to the vibrant nightlife of the community. She would never find a man way out here, her friends warned. Not when she was the youngest person on her block and the only eligible men came with dentures and support socks. Why not move to where the action was?

Laurel's answer was always the same. Those new builds didn't come with the character this house had. Hers came with original crown molding, exposed beams, and dozens of architectural details that modern construction couldn't emulate and, quite frankly, couldn't afford. She loved her rattling iron pipes and her squeaky wood floors. They echoed with history. They spoke of a simpler time and a gentler generation. She didn't need a kitchen with the latest everything. Her black appliances worked as well as stainless steel. Her house still had its original kitchen, its soapstone countertop older than she was but still in excellent condition. The enamel was chipped on the old farmhouse-style sink, but it came with a feature that the newer versions didn't: a tall back splash and a built-in drain board. She might not have the white subway tiles that were all the rage, but she liked her red brick. It gave her kitchen even more character.

Working in the emergency room was a stressful job, knowing her immediate actions could save or cost a person their life. Laurel didn't take that responsibility lightly. At the end of the day, she needed to relax and unwind, not go looking for a party. Bars and clubs held no appeal to this twenty-nine-year-old. Even on a Saturday night, give her a soaking tub and a good book, and she was recharged and ready for another day.

Stretched out in the long tub, soaking amid the scented bubbles, Laurel replayed the day's events in her mind. She prayed that Raul Gonzales pulled through, knowing that if he lived, his life would be forever changed. She thought of Block and Knuckles, admiring their close friendship but questioning their idea of fun. From what she picked up among their bits of coherent conversation, this was a regular occurrence for the semi-pro football players.

Her thoughts drifted to Lily and Harold. She couldn't help but wonder what their story was. Harold seemed like a normal enough teenager, bored spending his Saturday at the hospital, yet there had been something edgy about him, something Laurel couldn't quite put her finger on. It was more than just his poor manners and lack of appreciation.

Thinking of the red marks that would soon turn to a bruise upon his pale skin, she wondered if he was a victim of bullying. Worse yet, she couldn't ignore the possibility of abuse. Lily certainly didn't seem concerned with hurrying home to her other three children. It seemed that each time one test came back negative, the woman added a just-remembered ailment. To Laurel, it appeared that Lily was looking for an excuse to stay.

Maybe it's not just Harold who's abused. Maybe it's Lily, too, and that's why she doesn't want to go home.

That was one of the hardest parts of her job, seeing the lives some of her patients were forced to live, and being virtually powerless to help them.

But it seems to me, if she has other children at home, exposed to that same environment, she couldn't get back quickly enough. Wouldn't she want to protect them?

Laurel knew it was useless to try to understand the actions of others, particularly when it came to abusive relationships. People had their reasons for doing what they did, even if they made no sense to anyone but them. And as painful as it was to accept, Laurel couldn't help someone who wasn't ready for help.

Besides, who was she to judge? She had never been in an abusive relationship. She had never been a mother. She had never had to make an impossible choice, such as which child to protect over the other.

I could have it all wrong, she reminded herself. *Lily could just be a hypochondriac. Even though her tox screen came back normal, she could be looking for a chance to score some drugs. Harold may have taken a tumble playing a game of neighborhood hoops.* An image of his sun-deprived skin floated through her mind and Laurel scoffed at her own speculations. *Okay,* she acknowledged with a smirk, *more like he fell out of his gaming chair, kind of like our friend Block. A couple of red marks on a teenager doesn't necessarily mean a thing.*

Her mind danced around a dozen more thoughts, delaying the inevitable. Sooner or later, she knew it would come down to this. She knew she would end up thinking about Detective Cade Resnick. The handsome officer hadn't been far from her thoughts since she first saw him, even when she had been too busy to dwell on it.

Admit it, girl. You didn't just see him. You plowed into him like a blind donkey. Trouble is, fine racehorses can't be bothered with lowly donkeys.

The benefit of the old claw-foot tub wasn't just its size. Crafted from cast iron, it held the heat of the water long after the bubbles were gone. Before the temperature grew tepid, Laurel sank deeper into the watery depths and indulged in the memory of Cade's gorgeous brown eyes and that surprising smile as he left.

As happy as she was living by herself in her craftsman, she hoped to one day share it with a husband and, eventually, children. It wasn't something she thought about often, but it was always there, somewhere in the back of her mind. The last three years had been busy enough, moving back to the Bryan-College Station area, establishing her reputation in the local health care field, working her way up to Charge Nurse, and buying her first home. She was in no hurry to fill it, but some little crevice of her heart held a void. Maybe it was meeting Lily and imagining her struggles as a mother of four, or maybe it was the expectant mother with the false labor pains, but an old familiar ache had started up again. Maybe it had something to do with those brooding brown eyes, or maybe it was just that her heart had finally healed after Kenton. No matter the reason, for the first time in a long time, Laurel felt the whispery hands of her biological clock ticking.

"One day," she said aloud in the slowly cooling water. "One day, when you aren't even looking, you'll find the perfect man. Not perfect overall, but perfect for *you*. It's just a matter of time."

Pulling herself up from the waters, she dried off with a fluffy towel, slipped into her favorite gown, shook away thoughts of ticking clocks, empty hearts, and empty bedrooms, and went in search of something to eat. By the time she found a quick bite and cleaned up the kitchen, it was time for the evening news. She wanted to hear if they mentioned the hit and run accident involving Raul Gonzales, so she grabbed the remote and curled up on the sofa.

Second only to the lead story of the Aggie's come-back win at Kyle Field, the Gonzales story ran at the top of the newscast. The co-owner of the popular local restaurant chain was hit as he walked from the employee parking lot to the rear entrance of their downtown location. Surveillance cameras were down at the time of the accident and police had only a vague description of the vehicle suspected of hitting him. They were asking for anyone with information regarding the accident to call the number listed on the screen. At last report, Mr. Gonzales was undergoing a second surgery and was listed in critical condition at *Texas General.*

As the news moved on to the next story, Laurel yawned and turned off the television. Five-thirty would come early enough.

Laurel arrived at the hospital earlier than necessary, allowing plenty of time to make the transition from night shift to day shift. She reviewed the status of current patients, chatting with the outgoing team to bring herself up to speed. Before the last nurse left, she asked, "By the way, what time did Lily Moses finally get released?"

"Wasn't that the woman in Room 5, the one with the teenage son?" Cami St. John asked.

"Yes. Unexplained abdominal pain."

"We finally booked her in a room around midnight. Every time we thought she was stabilized and able to go home, she started screaming with pain. Her temp spiked at one point, and her heart rate was erratic."

A frown appeared on Laurel's face. "Almost the same thing while I was here. I just don't understand. All of her tests came back negative. Even Dr. Baek was stumped."

"So was Patterson. He finally decided the only way any of us would get any rest was to send her up to a room."

"Very strange," Laurel murmured. She made a mental note to check in with her later in the day. "Have you heard anything new on Mr. Gonzales?"

"From what I can tell, it's not looking good."

"I hope they catch whoever hit him."

"I know it won't change what's happened," Cami

agreed, "but at least it would be *something.*"

The siren's wail broke into their conversation. "Wow," Laurel said. "Not even seven-thirty on a Sunday morning, and it's already starting."

Cami, who had already signed out, offered a sympathetic look. "That was quite a game yesterday. The die-hard fans may have partied all night."

It was close to noon before Laurel had the opportunity to go upstairs and check on Lily. She found her dozing in the bed, her monitors registering normal numbers and no visible signs of distress. Not wanting to wake her, Laurel turned to go, until a scratchy voice stopped her.

"I'm awake."

"Sorry, I didn't mean to disturb you. I just wanted to see how you were doing."

"Okay, I guess. Doctors still can't tell me what's wrong." She straightened her slight form in the bed, making no more than a shallow bump beneath the covers.

"How did you rest last night?"

"Better than Harold. He fell off the couch yonder at least twice."

"Harold stayed all night?" Laurel asked in surprise. "Wow. What a trooper."

"Didn't have much choice. He don't drive."

"No one could come and get him?" Hearing the censure in her own voice, she made a show of looking around the room. "Where is he now?"

"I told him to go walk around. Find out the latest on that hit and run guy, the one they say owns the cafés around town, and all. We like to eat there on payday."

"Speaking of such, I never asked. Where do you work?"

"Housekeeping, over at *Maroon Motel*."

Laurel wasn't familiar with it, but she thought it might be a low-rent motel on Harvey Mitchell Parkway. She thought she remembered seeing a sign, tucked in behind the newer chain hotels.

"So?" Lily demanded. "How is he?"

Thrown by the change in topics, Laurel frowned. "How is who?"

"The restaurant guy! Did he make it through the last surgery?"

"I don't know any more than what the news is reporting, same as you."

"But you work here! You're a nurse, and all. They can tell you."

"Even if they did, I couldn't share that information with you. Or with anyone, for that matter."

Lily nibbled on the side of her finger. Laurel noticed that her nails were jagged and bitten off in the quick, the cuticles red and raw. "Are you worried about staying overnight in the hospital, Lily?" she guessed, her tone softening with compassion. No doubt, she worried about the three children left at home. "I'm sure it was simply an added precaution."

"I ain't worried about me. I just feel bad for that guy, and all."

A thought occurred to Laurel. "Do you know Mr. Gonzales personally?"

"No! No, of course not!" Lily looked down at her bed sheet, giving special care to pulling it in closer around her. "It just sounds like he might not make it, and all."

"He's getting the best possible care, I can assure you of that."

"That's good."

"Is there anything I can get for you, Lily? Anyone I

can call?"

"Nah. You can get someone to take my breakfast tray, if you want. I gave most of it to Harold, anyway." She pointed to the empty plate by her bedside.

"I know how hectic it can be, coming to the ER when you're in pain. If you got off without any money, I'd be happy to give Harold enough to eat on," Laurel offered, trying not to hurt the woman's pride with an offer of money.

"He's managing okay," Lily shrugged.

"You seem to be feeling better today. I'm so glad. Maybe you'll be released this afternoon."

"I don't know about that." Lily sounded uncertain, as her hand moved to her belly. A grimace moved across her face. "It still hurts something fierce."

"I'll speak to the nurses when I leave and see if they can do anything to make you more comfortable."

"Thanks, that'd be swell."

"Certainly. Again, if you need anything, just let me know."

"Thanks, Nurse Laurel." Lily gave her what looked like a genuine smile, timid though it was. "And if you hear anything on that guy…"

"I couldn't share it if I did," Laurel reminded her gently.

Lily knotted the sheet at her stomach. "It's just that it upset Harold, and all. Us coming in at the same time, and all."

"I can understand that. Let's just pray for the best. Are you sure there's nothing else I can do for you?"

"You might bring me a fresh washcloth to put on my forehead when I feel faint."

"Certainly." Laurel stepped into the adjoining bathroom to fetch a clean, cool cloth. 'Feeling faint' was a new ailment she hadn't heard before.

She heard the door swing open leading from the hall into Lily's room, and feet shuffling forward. Even before she heard his voice, she knew it was Harold. The teen didn't know how to walk without dragging his feet. But she had never heard him sound so aggravated—or animated—before now.

"That stupid detective! He's back again, asking Mama G all sorts of nosy questions! I think he suspects *her* of running over her old man!"

"Careful!" his mother warned sharply. "The nurse is in the bathroom. Uhm, don't hit her with the door, and all."

Laurel carefully poked her head out first, before stepping into the room. "Hello, Harold," she said with a smile. She lifted the washcloth in gesture as she carried it to Lily. "I was just getting this for your mom."

"Oh. Yeah. Yeah, hi." He looked startled to find her there. He shuffled forward, flinging himself onto the sofa that doubled as a bed.

"I couldn't help but overhear you say the detective is back again today?" She made it a question.

"Oh, uh, yeah. Yeah, I saw him while I was, uh, out walking around." He darted his eyes over toward his mom, obviously feeling guilty about getting caught wandering the halls. "You told me to go," he said defensively.

"You're not in trouble," Laurel said quickly. "I was just curious."

"Oh. Well, he acts like he thinks the wife had something to do with the accident. Which is stupid. I saw how she ran through the hall yesterday. She was ape shi—shivering crazy." He caught himself before saying something that would land him in trouble.

Laurel bit back a smile. "That she was. Hey. Do you like pizza? I have a craving for a meat lover's pie, but they don't make it in anything smaller than fourteen inches. None of the other nurses likes that kind, and I can't eat it all by myself. If I order one, would you be willing to help me out and eat most of it? I probably won't eat but one or two slices."

The teen shrugged nonchalantly, but she could have sworn she saw his mouth salivating at the mention of food. When the neck of his tee shirt slipped—the same worn out neckline from the day before—she saw the red marks had darkened into a definite bruise, making her wonder, once again, what had caused them.

"I guess I could eat a bite or two."

"Great! I'll order as soon as I get back to my desk."

"Sure, whatever."

"Let me just grab this empty tray, and I'll get out of your way. Lily, don't forget to call me if you need anything. You, too, Harold."

CHAPTER FIVE

After depositing the empty tray and inquiring at the nurses' station about Lily, Laurel decided to check in on Mr. Gonzales. She knew she wasn't privy to personal information, but she wanted to check on his status and offer encouragement to Esmeralda, even if she was a bit of a wifezilla.

Esmeralda was in the family waiting room of ICU, talking on her cell phone. Laurel took a moment to assess her before approaching.

Dressed moderately more sedate in black leggings, colorful top, two-inch heels. Still towers over me by several inches. Hair styled, make-up impeccable, diamonds shined. Looks amazingly rested after a restless night in the hospital waiting room. Unless, of course, she didn't stay the night.

Esmeralda Gonzales spoke in Spanish, so Laurel had no idea what she said or with whom she spoke, but she needed no translator to understand the words were a sharp reprimand. Her limited knowledge of Spanish picked up a few phrases: *chico estupido* (stupid boy), *no importa* (never mind), *idiota* (idiot), and *terminado para mañana* (finished by tomorrow.)

Laurel hung back, trying to respect the woman's privacy, but Esmeralda noticed her anyway. A look of aggravation crossed her face, mingled with something akin to guilt.

She probably feels guilty tending business while her husband's life hangs in the balance, Laurel thought, *but I doubt the demands of owning three restaurants ever ceases, even at a time like this.*

Esmeralda turned her head to bark out a few parting words and a terse *adios.* With something that looked more like a grimace than a smile, she faced Laurel with a perfunctory nod of acknowledgment. "Nurse."

"Hello, Mrs. Gonzales. I'm not sure you remember me, but I'm Laurel Benson. We met—"

She interrupted her with a stiff, "I remember you."

Laurel pushed on, despite the chilly reception. "I don't mean to disturb you, but I wanted to see if I could help in any way. Can I bring you anything?"

"Can you bring me two good legs for my husband?"

"As a matter of fact—"

Before she could tout the amazing progress made with modern prosthetics, the other woman interrupted her again. "No, you cannot. No one can do this for my Raul."

"How is he?" Laurel asked in a soft voice.

"Barely clinging to life. Once he hears he is not a whole man, he will not wish to live."

Laurel knew that now was not the time to correct the distraught wife. Keeping a positive attitude was crucial for patient recovery, and Esmeralda shouldn't think in terms of her husband not being "whole." Even if the rumors were true and they were planning to divorce, how Esmeralda responded to his injuries could be huge in Raul's healing process.

"I'm so sorry." She knew it was best to keep her response simple and sincere.

"Such a stupid, needless accident. *Ridículo.*"

"Yes, ridiculous," Laurel sympathized. "Is there anything I can do for you?"

Pursing her painted lips in thought, Esmeralda contemplated the offer for only a moment before saying, "Yes! Keep that inept detective away from me. If he continues to bother me with his silly questions, I will sue him—and the hospital—for harassment!"

"I'm afraid we have no control over an official police investigation," Laurel pointed out. "Don't you want justice for your husband? I'm sure they are simply trying to do a thorough job and investigate from every angle."

"Then he should be on the street, looking for the blue car that hit Raul, not asking me about my finances! I have no time for such useless questions."

She was making no promises, but Laurel murmured, "I'll see what I can do."

"You do that." Esmeralda turned her head away with a brush of her hand. "I would like to be alone now."

"Certainly. I wish you and your husband the best."

Laurel blew out a tense breath as she walked away. The woman certainly hadn't made her offer of condolence easy, or particularly pleasant. *At least I tried,* she consoled herself, *with both Esmeralda and Lily.*

An hour and a half later, Laurel carved out a few minutes to return to the floor, this time with a large meat lover's pizza in tow. She took out a slice for herself but brought the remainder to the skinny teen on the second floor.

The door to Lily's room was partially open when she arrived, and Laurel could hear she had a guest. Her momentary pleasure at thinking someone cared enough to visit was crushed when she heard the heated conversation on the other side of the door.

"I gave you half the money!" Lily hissed in anger. "What more do you want?"

"The other half!" a man's rough voice snarled.

"You'll get your money."

"When?" the man demanded.

"Soon. It can't be much longer now."

"The boss needs a definite date. Here's a hint. Anything over ten days is too long."

"Fine!" Lily hurled the word. "I'll have the money in ten days. Then I never want to see your ugly face again!"

"No problem."

The door jerked open and a man stormed out. Despite his small, wiry build, Laurel knew he wasn't the kind of man to be crossed. *Full sleeve tattoo, some dark swirl of evil-looking devils and snakes curling together to slither up his arm and wind around his neck. Good pecs, obviously in good physical condition. Bald head is more of a power statement than a health ailment, judging from the single strip of dreadlocks down the center. High tolerance to pain, if all that ink and those gold hoops and diamonds studs are any indication.* An overabundance of jewelry adorned the curve of each ear from top to bottom. More gold glittered on his knuckles, and when he offered Laurel a sleazy smile, she saw the flash of a diamond embedded in one tooth.

She shivered in spite of herself. If this were the minion, she would hate to cross paths with "the boss." She was even reluctant to retrace this man's trail in and out of Lily's room, irrational though it was. She waited until the count of three, allowing the negative vibes to dissipate before knocking. Even though the door stood open, she waited at the threshold.

"Lily? May I come in? I brought a pizza for Harold."

There was the sound of shuffled feet, a creaking mattress, and a decided sniff. "Yeah," Lily finally said. "Come in."

Pasting on a smile, Laurel walked into a room heavy with tension. Harold huddled into one corner of the couch, his face paler than normal, and for once, Lily looked truly ill. Her face was pinched and pale, and there was an angry red circle around her wrist. A glance at the monitor said her heart rate and blood pressure were both sky-high. Amid the beeping alarms, Laurel tried to diffuse the tense situation.

"Here you go, Harold. One meat lover's pizza, as promised." She sat the aromatic box down with a flourish. Resetting the alarm on the monitor, she asked Lily if she felt all right.

"Hurtin' a bit," she said.

Laurel decided not to mention the visitor. Instead, she spoke to Harold. "I really appreciate you taking this off my hands. I hated to see it go to waste, but I just can't eat it all by myself."

"No prob," the teen said, but his enthusiasm was lackluster. Laurel suspected their unwanted guest had spoiled his appetite.

"I have to run, but I hope you enjoy the pizza. Since your mom is experiencing abdominal pain, you probably shouldn't share with her."

"Don't worry," Lily said in a sharp voice. "I ain't hungry."

Laurel paused when she reached the door. "You know," she mentioned casually, "if you're getting too many visitors and it's wearing you out, we can always put a 'Do Not Disturb' sign on your door."

"I'll remember that."

Laurel stepped from the room, wondering how Lily

and her son were tangled up with *that* man. She sighed heavily, knowing that sometimes, there was simply nothing she could do to help a patient. Turning onto the corridor that led to the elevators, she saw the man from earlier standing near the elevator, talking on his cellphone. She stepped back quickly, not wanting him to see her. She didn't even try to hear what was being said; she wanted nothing to do with the man and his nefarious business.

She could always use the elevators on the other side of the wing. Not daring to see if he was still there, Laurel looked straight ahead as she walked past the corridor where the man had been and headed toward the south end of the second floor. Even before she reached the ICU wing, she could hear loud voices coming from the waiting area.

"What is the meaning of this?" she cried, rounding the corner. "Please remember that you are in a hospital!" Busy making her reprimand, she didn't notice, at first, who she chided.

"I told you to keep this man away from me!" Esmeralda Gonzales stormed, pointing a long fingernail at a man in a dark gray western-cut jacket.

When the man turned, Laurel saw that it was Cade Resnick. Her heart did a silly little somersault, and the frown on her face wavered. Seeing her, the detective crooked an eyebrow, as if mocking her authority over him.

Laurel addressed the woman first. "As I told you, Mrs. Gonzales, the hospital makes every effort to cooperate with an official police investigation." To make certain the detective was clear on her stance, Laurel put her hands onto her hips and turned to look him squarely the eye. "If Mrs. Gonzales were one of my patients, it might be another matter. But as she is a guest, I can't interfere with your line of questioning. I can, however, insist that you both keep your voices down or take this discussion elsewhere."

Appearing amused by her bravado, the detective resisted the smile tickling the edges of his mouth. It earned him a glare from the petite nurse, until he gave a cordial nod and relented. "I do apologize for having this heated discussion here. It won't happen again."

Laurel held his gaze for a solid moment, unwavering in her resolve. "See that it doesn't."

With that, she marched off.

By the time she reached the other set of elevators, the detective was immediately behind her. He leaned close to reach around her and push the *Down* arrow.

"Hello again, Nurse Benson," he said.

"Hello." She kept the greeting short and terse, relaying her irritation in a single utterance.

"I do apologize about that," he said. When the doors slid open, a family of four exited. With a wave of his hand, the officer motioned for Laurel to enter first.

The elevator was too small for her and all that testosterone. It bounced around the confines of the four walls, hitting her from every direction. His woodsy cologne had the same effect on her as yesterday, coupled now with the memory of his devastating smile.

"Why on earth were you having a shouting match with the wife of an ICU patient?" She whirled to confront him, thankful he didn't wear that smile now. If anything, he looked increasingly unhappy with her as she flung the words at him. On a roll, she continued, "Particularly when he is in such grave condition? Couldn't your inquiry wait?"

The lines around his mouth tightened. No smile in

sight now. "Obviously, if I felt it could wait, it would have. I'm not completely insensitive, you know."

"No, I don't know!" she flung back at him, crossing her arms over her waist.

"In situations like this," he informed her coolly, "it's imperative to act on every lead, as quickly as they come in. It often means the difference in solving a crime or letting someone get away scot-free."

"You do understand that her husband may very well die. His injuries are extensive."

"All the more reason to press forward," he insisted stubbornly. "If Raul Gonzales dies, it becomes a murder investigation."

The doors slid open and a couple started to step inside. "Going down?" the man asked pleasantly. One look at Detective Resnick's thunderous expression, and he withdrew his foot. "Uhm, we'll wait," he said, stepping back.

It wasn't until the doors closed again that Cade realized they had never punched a button. He jabbed the glowing "1" with a quick motion.

Laurel hadn't considered the murder aspect, and it gave her pause. Relenting the tiniest of bits, she asked, "And you think the wife is somehow involved?"

An emotion flickered across the detective's face, which he quickly squelched. "I'm not at liberty to discuss an ongoing investigation."

"But the spouse is always the first suspect, right?"

"Generally speaking, yes," he allowed.

Laurel twisted her mouth in thought. "And they are going through a divorce."

He looked at her curiously, as the car came to a stop. Before the doors opened, he asked, "How do you know that?"

"Actually, one of my patients yesterday mentioned it. She's a patron of their restaurants and said they are fighting over who gets control of their newest location."

"Mrs. Gonzales led me to believe that she had changed her mind."

Laurel stepped out as the doors opened. "No idea. I'm just going by what the girl told me."

"Okay, then," he said, hinting that his job just became more complicated. They walked together toward the front, where Laurel suspected they would part ways.

Well ahead of them, the man from Lily's room exited the other set of elevators and went out the front entrance. Beside her, Detective Resnick muttered through a dark scowl, "What is Icepick doing here?"

"Who is that man?" Laurel asked. "I saw him upstairs earlier."

"He is bad news with a capital B. He works for a known loan shark here in town, with suspected ties to a major crime syndicate. They call him Icepick because of his preferred method of persuasion. Whatever you do, do not tangle with that man."

A shiver moved through Laurel's body. *What is Lily involved in?* she wondered.

"Where did you see him?" he asked. "What was he doing?"

"He was coming out of a patient's room," she said. For some reason, she was reluctant to mention Lily's name.

"Like I said, steer clear of that man."

"Believe me, I will. In fact," she admitted with a sheepish smile, "that's why I came down the ICU hallway. I didn't want to share an elevator with him."

"Wise choice."

As they reached the corridor leading to the ER, Laurel

found her feet slowing. As aggravating as the man was, she hated to say goodbye. She might never see him again, and the thought left her oddly bereft.

Cade matched his steps to hers. His voice sounded sincere as he said, "I really am sorry about earlier. I didn't mean to get in a shouting match with Mrs. Gonzales, but she can be a very stubborn woman."

A smile played around Laurel's mouth. "Nothing wrong with that," she said, making a show of not meeting his eyes.

"I sense it's a common ailment around here," he said, almost in a teasing manner. He leaned in as he said it, offering another hint of his woodsy cologne.

Is he flirting with me? The possibly quickened her heart rate and made her feet clumsy.

"I don't suppose you have any of that shrimp-avocado dip left, do you?" he asked hopefully. "I've been craving that all morning."

She pretended to be aghast, putting her hand to her chest. "Don't tell me you're pregnant!"

His laugh was genuine, and had a devastating effect on Laurel's equilibrium. "Hardly!" he hooted. When he noticed her faltered step, he thrust a hand out to steady her.

A bit belated, she knew, but Laurel darted a quick glance to his ring finger. *No tan line*, she noticed gratefully. She would hate to make a fool of herself over another woman's husband. It was bad enough behaving so foolishly over an eligible man! Her face heated with her clumsiness.

"You still have my card?" he asked. "Just in case?"

She didn't trust herself to speak and walk at the same time, so she merely nodded.

"I guess I'll see you later, then, Nurse Benson," he

said.

She managed a reminder. "Laurel."

There it was again, that surprisingly easy smile. "That's right," he said, the smile spreading across his handsome face. "Laurel."

He gave her arm a small squeeze before releasing it.

Do not stumble, she told herself as she walked away. *Put one foot in front of the other, nice and steady. Don't do anything stupid, because you know he's watching you. Walk away nice and slow, like you don't have a care in the world.*

She reached the department doors without incident, but once on the other side, her shoulders sagged and her feet forgot how to move.

If this is your reaction to a hot guy flirting with you, you are in sad shape, Miss Benson. Sad shape, indeed.

CHAPTER SIX

When Cade returned to the police station, the desk officer caught his attention.

"Detective Resnick, I put a note on your desk," Donna Israel said, covering the mouthpiece as she held the phone to her ear. "The one from a Mr. Miller, about a burglary."

"Turn it over to the Theft Unit, Donna. I'm up to my eyeballs in the Gonzales case."

"Believe me; you're going to want to take this one."

With a frown, Cade waited for more explanation, but she had gone back to her call. Huffing out a sigh, he proceeded to his desk, where more than just a single note awaited him. There had to be at least a dozen, which only irritated him more. He shuffled through them until he found the one in question.

"What is this about, Israel?" he yelled, ignoring the fact she was still on the phone.

"Stolen blue Chevrolet," she called back.

Interest piqued, he dialed the number listed. An elderly man answered on the third ring.

"Mr. Miller? This is Detective Cade Resnick with the

College Station Police. I understand—"

"Yes, yes, I've been waiting for your call," the man interrupted. "Are you on your way over?"

"No, sir, not yet. Can you tell me more about the reason for your call?"

"Like I told the lady on the phone, someone stole my car yesterday."

"And you're just now reporting it?"

"Just now noticed."

The caller couldn't see him roll his eyes. "Did you provide an accurate description and license plate number? If we hope to get it back—"

Once again, the older man interrupted him. "I've already got it back, Detective."

Cade found his temper rising. He had better things to do than take calls from crackpots, even if they did sound like perfectly nice elderly gentlemen. "Mr. Miller, if you have your car back, I really don't understand why you reported it missing."

"If you'd come over, you'd know exactly why I called."

Cade huffed out a sigh. "I'll try to send a unit—"

"Did I mention," the old man interrupted again, "I think it was the car that hit that Gonzales guy?"

"I'll be right over."

Fifteen minutes later, Cade pulled up to a well-maintained older home in an established neighborhood. Sure enough, a '75 Chevy Monte Carlo sat under the carport. According to the few reports they had managed to garner, a similar older model, light-blue car had hit Raul Gonzales.

A stooped man wearing sagging pants with suspenders and colorful argyle socks waited beside the vehicle.

After exchanging introductions, Cade turned to the car. "This the car?"

"Sure is. Belonged to my late wife Betty. Still runs like the day it rolled off the assembly line," he boasted.

"And why do you believe it was stolen yesterday, Mr. Miller? Do you have any idea of the time it was taken? Or returned?"

"I'm not senile yet, if that's what you're thinking," the older man said. "I took the car down to Whataburger for my morning coffee. Parked it around noon, came in to make lunch and watch the game. Did you happen to catch it? It was nail biter, it was!"

"No, sir, I had to work," Cade answered politely, waiting for the conversation to circle back around to the theft.

"I stayed inside the rest of the day, so I don't know what time they took it. Truth is, after such an exciting game, I was all tuckered out. Fell asleep in my recliner until it was time for my evening shows. I like to watch that one about the guys who fix up old cars and give them to vets. You ever watch that one?"

Cade's smile was tight. He was beginning to wonder if the old man hadn't called simply because he was lonely. It wouldn't be the first time. "Can't say that I have."

"You should watch it sometime. It's a good show, and a fine way to honor our soldiers."

Trying to pull the older man back on track, Cade asked, "And you didn't hear anything coming from the carport? No engines starting? Your own, maybe?"

"Nah, she hums along as quiet as a mouse," he bragged. "Even without the TV going, it's hard to hear this little darlin'. With it on, it's impossible. Which explains why I never heard a thing, even when they brought her back."

"And when do you think that was?"

He shrugged his hunched shoulders. "Sometime before the paper lady threw the Sunday paper. You can see it there, on the hood. I left it be, so you could see for yourself."

Just as he said, the thick coil showed just enough of the *Bryan Eagle* banner with the day's date to confirm the current edition.

"So why do you believe your car was stolen, Mr. Miller? And why do you believe it was used in the hit and run accident involving Mr. Gonzales?"

Wally Miller stood back and made a flourishing motion with his arms. "Just see for yourself," he invited.

Cade moved to inspect the front of the vehicle. Whatever doubts he harbored vanished when he saw the crumpled front bumper all but scraping the ground. Its once shiny chrome bore dark streaks, no doubt blood. The hood and right front fender had heavy damage, but the most telling evidence was the swatch of material still snagged in the grill. Unless he was sorely mistaken, the color was consistent with the clothes Gonzales had been wearing.

Cade immediately pulled out his phone and snapped a few photos before dialing the station. As he waited for the line to pick up, he asked, "Mr. Miller, can anyone vouch for you yesterday between the times of two and three p.m.?"

"What do you mean?"

"Was anyone here with you, watching the game?"

The older man narrowed his eyes. "Just what are you asking?"

"Can anyone substantiate your claim that you weren't driving the car during the time of the accident?"

"Now, wait a minute, young fella. I called you out so

you could see the damage to the car and so I could help find the coward that hit Mr. G. I didn't call you out here to insult me and call me a liar to my face!" The old man's face turned red as he pointed a gnarled finger in Cade's direction.

The line connected and Cade barked instructions into the phone, calling for a forensic team. He gave a brief description of his findings and what he needed. When he disconnected and turned back to the old man, he found that he had collapsed on the ground, clutching at his chest.

When the paramedics came, Cade couldn't say why, but he instinctively directed them to *Texas General.*

"Possible heart attack! Blood pressure 198/100. Heart rate unsteady with significant ST elevation."

Laurel grabbed a crash cart and met the medics in Room 5. The next thirty minutes were a blur, but the crisis finally passed and Mr. Miller was stable. She wearily retreated to the break room for a quick respite.

She was still at the table, nursing a cup of hot tea, when Detective Resnick found her.

"Detective," she said in surprise. She quickly set her feet back on the floor and straightened her crooked scrub top. She didn't bother with her hair. "What are you doing back here? Do you have a break in the case?"

"Yes and no. And, please. Don't disturb yourself on my account." Without asking permission, he took hold of her legs and raised them back to their former resting place in the seat of the next chair. Laurel would have protested, if her voice hadn't failed her.

"Th—Thanks," she managed to stammer. "Please. Have a seat."

He took the chair across the table from her, so that they were facing.

"I'm guessing you attended Mr. Miller."

Again, surprise filled her face. "You know him?"

"We met this afternoon. I'm the one who called the ambulance."

"Oh. Well, you called just in time. We were able to administer immediate care, and it looks like he'll come through nicely."

"That's good to hear."

Noticing the solemn look on his face, Laurel frowned. "You don't look very pleased."

How did he explain that he might have to arrest her patient for vehicular assault? If the patient died, it could escalate to vehicular manslaughter. He settled on a partial truth.

"The fact is, I was investigating a crime involving Mr. Miller—or at least his car—when he had his heart attack."

"Hmm. That might explain some of his rambling," Laurel mused.

"Like what?"

"He kept apologizing to someone named Betty."

"His late wife," Cade supplied.

"And something about trying to do the right thing." She cocked her head, still not certain about the next part. "I can't be sure, but I thought he kept saying Mr. G. But that's crazy, right?"

When Cade's only reply was a solemnly drawn deep breath, Laurel's eyes widened. "You mean… it was *his* car that hit Mr. Gonzales?" she gasped.

The detective looked conflicted. "I'm not at liberty to say. But yes, I have reason to believe his vehicle could have been involved."

"Surely you don't think that nice old man did this! He's been nothing but sweet and apologetic for causing so much fuss."

"I doubt he intentionally ran the man over, but there's a good possibility he could have done so accidentally. He's over eighty, you know."

"That doesn't make him automatically guilty!" Laurel bristled, thinking of her own grandfather. He still drove his faithful old '69 Ford truck. Both had seen a lot of years and a lot of miles. In the detective's eyes, did that make PeePaw a criminal, as well?

A frown marred Cade's face. "Of course not. But at his age, the vision and the reflexes aren't what they once were."

"So? You're going to arrest the poor man while he's lying in the hospital?"

Cade didn't understand why the nurse was so upset. He also didn't understand why he chose now to notice the little flecks of color in her hazel eyes. The green was particularly prominent, brought out by the color of her scrubs and alive with the glow of irritation. Electricity zapped from her heated stare.

Pushing his irrational attraction to this fireball aside, Cade's voice came out terse. "I never mentioned arresting him." *Thought it, yes. Never said it out loud.* The disclaimer ran through his mind, even as his face remained stoic.

"Is that why you're still here?" Laurel asked coldly. It nettled her, knowing she wasted valuable tub-time fantasizing about a man with no regard for the elderly. Who knew such a cold heart hid behind those warm brown eyes? She put an added dose of venom to her words. "Waiting for him to wake up, so you can read him his rights?"

Again, his brow puckered. "What am I missing here? Are you friends with Mr. Miller?"

"I just met him thirty minutes ago, but yes, I would be pleased to call him my friend." A slight toss of dark curls punctuated her reply.

"Why are you so defensive of a man you've known less than an hour? For all either of us know about the man, he could be a hitman, hired to take Gonzales out."

"Seriously? At eighty?" Laurel hooted.

"In case you don't know, being eighty doesn't pay so well," Detective Resnick told her smugly. "He could have insurmountable debts and felt this was the only way out. You don't know him. Certainly not well enough to defend him."

"Maybe not," she conceded, "but I know that his age doesn't automatically make him a suspect."

"No, but owning the car that hit our victim and having no alibi for the time of the crime does."

"Even *you* said it could have been unintentional," Laurel reminded him. "That doesn't make it a crime, just a tragic accident."

"You're right. But leaving the scene of an accident and failing to report it definitely *is* a crime."

Laurel refused to give up so easily. "How did you know about his car?" she challenged.

With only slight hesitation, Cade admitted, "He called and reported that his car had been stolen."

"Aha! So he *did* report it!"

"A day later. And only after a description of the vehicle was released to the public, urging anyone seeing a similar car to report it."

"But if it was stolen…"

"It was still parked under his carport."

Laurel had no quick reply for this bit of information.

Brows knitted, she nibbled on her lip in thought. "How far does he live from the scene of the crime?"

"A few blocks."

"So, someone could have stolen his car, used it to hit Mr. Gonzales, and returned it to its original spot. Correct?"

Clearly reluctant, Cade grunted out a yes. "That's what he's claiming," he continued, "but he has no alibi for the time in question. I owe it to Raul Gonzales to check out the possibility that your friend is hiding the truth. He could have unintentionally hit Mr. Gonzales, panicked, and driven home to hide the evidence, only to have a change of heart the next day. We simply don't know." He leveled that gorgeous brown gaze upon her. "But it's my job, Nurse Benson, to find out what really happened."

"I do understand that," Laurel relented, her voice somewhat softer. Her eyes took on that glow again. The flame of her determination was even brighter and more intense than the former glow of irritation. "However, it is *my* job to protect the health of my patient. I can't allow you to upset him and cause him distress during this critical point in his recovery."

"And just this afternoon, you claimed the hospital made every attempt to cooperate with a police investigation," he mocked her.

"We do. But I also told you that if it were my patient, I might have a different take. Which Mr. Miller is, and which I do." Laurel pushed up from the table and stood at her full five feet, four inches to glare down at him. "You're on my territory now, Detective. And I will not allow you to badger my patient."

"I have no intentions of badgering him. I simply want to ask a few more questions for my investigation."

Laurel stood her ground. "It will have to wait."

The light that came to his dark eyes wasn't nearly as fascinating as the light shining from hers. If anything, it was rather frightening. Laurel made a mental note that Cade Resnick was a staunch and committed lawman, and not someone to cross. She wouldn't relish being on his bad side, if that light of determination was any indication of his dedication.

"I'm a patient man," he said. The low timber of his voice could as easily be a threat, as much as a promise.

She crossed her arms, lifting her chin in defiance. "Then it appears we are at a crossroads, Detective."

"I suppose maybe we are, Nurse." He pushed up from his chair, almost ten inches taller than she was. His height, alone, was imposing. "But I have a job to do, and I intend to do it."

"As do I."

"Fine."

"Fine."

They engaged in a battle of the stare, neither of them willing to back down.

Stop noticing how deliciously brown his eyes are! Laurel hissed to herself. *Doesn't matter if he's the best-looking thing you've seen in a month of Sundays. He'd arrest PeePaw, given half the chance. Ignore the crazy beat of your heart and concentrate on Mr. Miller's. That's what's important here, not those eyes and those shoulders and that cocky little crook of his eyebrows. Gotta outrun the Testosterone Man.*

They would never know who might have won that day. Mary Ann skidded to a halt in the doorway, her voice breathless above the sounding alarms. "Three car pile-up, multiple injuries. You're needed."

Without another word, Laurel whirled and followed her friend. Her petty showdown with the detective paled in comparison to patients in need.

Once she was out of sight, Cade broke out in a grin. He wasn't amused by news of another accident, but Nurse Benson thoroughly and charmingly amused him. There was something about her that he found intriguing.

Not, mind you, that he was looking for a woman. His career kept him more than busy. In his so-called "spare time", he worked on the ranch and team roped with his best friend Shane. Pursuing a woman was so far down on Cade's to-do list that it barely warranted a thought. Maybe someday—in the far, far future, of course—he would consider finding a woman and settling down. Maybe. But not now, and certainly not like this. He'd look for a woman with similar interests and a softer demeanor. Someone he could laugh with, not someone he argued with at every turn.

Yet, looking or not, Laurel Benson amused him. However, being amused by a woman and being attracted to one were two very different things, he assured himself.

Okay, Cade relented, if only to himself. *So maybe in this case, they are the same.*

After all, she was quite pretty, and he certainly wasn't blind. And while some men might be deterred by her fiery temper and sharp tongue, he found them refreshingly unique. Both sparked easily when it came to her job, which only showed her passion for her career and for her patients. Was it so wrong to admire that in a woman?

No, he firmly decided. He liked that about her.

The fact was, he liked *her*.

He liked her *a lot*.

The amusement on his face died. Considering their recent stare-off and the jobs they both had to do, that could be a problem.

CHAPTER SEVEN

Not all Mondays were doomed. Laurel had the day off, so for her, the day shaped up nicely.

She ran errands early in the afternoon. When she found herself near the downtown location of *Mama G's*, she couldn't resist stopping in for a late lunch.

The *taqueria* was a no-frills establishment, with orders taken at the counter and delivered to the table. At Carly Acosta's suggestion, Laurel ordered the fish tacos and found a booth with a window view near the back of the building. It overlooked the parking lot, but a trellis with colorful peppers growing against it made a nice distraction. While she waited for her food, a worker stepped outside, plucked a few of the offerings from the vines, and dropped them into a shallow pan.

Liking the idea of fresh peppers in her food, Laurel developed a new appreciation for Esmeralda and Raul Gonzales.

She watched as the worker paused to gaze beyond the trellis. Seeing the shiver that ran through the young woman's shoulders, Laurel followed her line of vision. That was when she noticed the chalk and paint markings on the asphalt outside.

That must be where it happened. Literally, right outside the door. How sad. And how brazen. Anyone sitting in this booth could have seen the entire thing unfold. Laurel wondered if that was how the police had a description of the car.

Before a certain pair of delicious brown eyes could derail her thoughts, Laurel forced herself to study the scene outside. The handrail laid in splinters on the ground, apparently the only barrier between Raul Gonzales and the impact of the car. Unfortunately for the restaurateur, it hadn't been enough. Last she heard, his condition was downgraded to grave.

"Here you go," the server said as she delivered the tray. "Two fish tacos and our special cilantro-dill sauce."

"Mmm. Looks yummy. I hear they're delicious." Laurel rubbed her hands together eagerly before taking the tray. "By the way. What's the latest on Mr. Gonzales? That was terrible what happened to him!"

The woman's face sagged. "Pure tragedy," she clucked. "We're still in shock. Things aren't looking good for our Mr. G, I'm afraid." Dipping her gray head, she made the sign of a cross over her chest.

"Have you worked here long?"

"Since day one," she boasted. "This location is the original, and opened in 1994. I've been with them every step of the way."

"Were you working that day?" No need to specify what day she meant.

"*Si.* Game Days are all hands on deck. I was serving this very table when we heard the racket. I looked up in time to see a light blue car, going lickity-split right past this window! For a minute there, it wobbled, and I thought it would come crashing through the wall. They were driving like a bat out of Hades!" She used her hands to indicate the speed.

The lively rendition sent a chill through Laurel. "Did you see who was driving?"

"All I saw was a streak of blue car and maybe a gray shirt inside. It was just a blur of movement. And then someone screamed, and we saw Mr. G laying there on the ground." Her whole body shook with revulsion and she crossed herself again. "Horrible."

"And Mrs. G?" Laurel stretched her neck, searching for a glimpse of the woman in the busy establishment. "Has she been in? How is she holding up?"

"Mama G? The woman is a rock. She's been here every day, looking in on things, even with her husband lying at death's door."

"I suppose the normalcy of the job grounds her," Laurel murmured. "Maybe that's where she gets her strength."

The older woman practically spat with disgust. "When I say rock, I don't mean strong. I mean hard and cold. Nothing comes between Mama G and her almighty dollar." She tapped the table as she turned. "Enjoy your fish tacos."

Laurel pondered the woman's statement as she arranged her plate and utensils. The picture she painted hardly fit the hysterical woman she had seen in the hospital. But Laurel knew, perhaps better than most, how visits to the ER often brought out the true nature of a person, good or bad. Perhaps Esmeralda Gonzales had a softer side that she kept hidden from her employees.

As Laurel bit into her taco, all thoughts of Mama G fled. Just as Carly Acosta predicted, they did, indeed, blow her mind.

After devouring every bite of her food and making a

note to come here again, Laurel stopped by her favorite fresh produce stand on the way home. She wanted to pick up a few pumpkins for her front porch and set the mood for what the calendar said was early October. Autumn was such a fleeting time in Texas, many people joked that it lasted no more than a single afternoon. Most years, the temperatures soared into the high eighties and even nineties in October; November was often only slightly more pleasant.

There was the occasional cool front, of course, when the heat subsided and there was a decided chill in the morning air. At the first hint of cooler weather, Texans pulled out their sweaters and hoodies, hoping to need them before January. Experience trained them not to stow away their flip-flops and sleeveless shirts until Thanksgiving or after, but there was something comforting in the mere *promise* of cooler weather. A hint was all it took for the fall decor to come out and the pumpkin spice lattes to flow. By the time the leaves actually changed color and the days were markedly cooler, the Christmas decorations were already in full force. That was why the calendar dictated fall decorating, not the weather.

Her phone rang as she selected her pumpkins and a basketful of Indian corn. Lodging the phone under her chin, she continued filling her shopping cart as she answered.

"Hello, Miz Paula. What can I do for you?"

"Hello, dear," their scheduling coordinator greeted. "I'm sorry to disturb you on your day off, but I'm in a bit of a bind. One of our nurses went into labor and we're short-handed tomorrow. Would you by chance be interested in filling in?"

Laurel mentally ran through her plans for tomorrow.

Laundry and more laundry.

"I think I could manage it," she agreed, all the time knowing she was a push over. She seldom turned anyone down when they asked her to work an extra shift.

"Wonderful! You'll be on the floor, in case I didn't say. Thanks, love. You're a lifesaver."

That's because I don't have a life of my own. A surly frown curled Laurel's lip as she pushed her cart to the checkout stand, but it vanished as she greeted the cashier and paid for her purchases. *On the bright side, I can check in on Mr. Miller, not to mention Mr. G.*

She refused to acknowledge the tiny flare of hope that her path might cross with that of a certain persistent detective. No, she stubbornly decided, the spring in her step was *definitely* from the pumpkins.

Being that *Texas General* was a small, independently owned hospital, it only housed fifty-plus beds. Today, Laurel worked on the second floor, caring for Med-Surg patients. It was a nice change from ER, although not necessarily any slower. Some of their patients could be quite needy and quick with the call button.

As expected, Lily Moses went home the day before. From what Laurel gathered, they were no closer to a diagnosis for her 'terrible bad' pain than when she first came in. Even the second-floor nurses suspected the woman hid some ulterior motive for staying overnight or was, at best, a hypochondriac. Laurel hoped for the latter.

She was surprised to find Mr. Miller moved to a room. Laurel dropped by to check on him and found that he was in excellent spirits. However, the doctor wanted to run more tests and to keep an eye on him for a few days before allowing him to return home. Visiting with him only reinforced Laurel's belief that he was a kind, elderly man who couldn't possibly have been involved in Raul Gonzales's accident.

Around noon, word reached Laurel that Mr. Gonzales had succumbed to his extensive injuries and died. Esmeralda Gonzales wasn't there at the time, but there was no mistaking when she did arrive. It was about ten minutes after the time of death, but everyone on the second floor could hear her wails of distress. After a litany of prayer and pleading, her sorrow turned to wrath. For another ten minutes, she screamed obscenities to the hospital and all staff who dared approach, threatening lawsuits and curses from the devil. A family member finally convinced her to leave, but not before security was forced to intervene and a doctor administered a sedative.

Laurel made an extra round to patients' rooms, quietly checking to make certain her drama had not adversely affected them. One woman was visibly shaken, certain the same fate would come to her. Laurel stayed and visited for a while, until the woman relaxed enough to take a nap.

Her next stop was Mr. Miller's room. "Just checking in on you," she chirped, poking her dark head inside the doorway.

"That was quite a racket out there," the elderly man agreed, "but understandable. How old was her boy?"

"It was her husband who passed away, not her son," Laurel corrected, taking the question as encouragement to come inside.

"The way she kept saying mama, I figured it was her son."

Fully into the room now, Laurel saw that Mr. Miller

wasn't alone. A surge of pleasure flashed through her when she saw the handsome detective seated near the bed, but she quickly shot it down. Judging from the notepad in his hand, he was there for an interrogation.

"What are *you* doing here?" she demanded.

"Just having a little visit with Mr. Miller here," Cade explained. His demeanor was casual, as if this were nothing more than a social visit.

Laurel knew better. "I won't have you upsetting my patient," she warned. Her eyes flashed with that fire that Cade found so intriguing.

"I have no intentions of upsetting him. We're simply having a nice little chat."

Laurel would have continued to glare at the detective, but the tiny smile playing around the edges of his mouth was very distracting. His dark eyes held a glimmer of mirth. She didn't think he was laughing *at* her, per se, but he definitely found something amusing. With a toss of her loose curls, she directed her attention to her patient.

"Is this true, Mr. Miller?"

"This young man and I are talking cars. I have a real beaut, you know. A '75 Chevy Monte Carlo Landau in mint condition. Runs like a dream."

He didn't mention the recent damage, which had Laurel casting her eyes back to Cade. His only reply was a slight shake of the head. She couldn't tell if that was disappointment in his eyes, or sympathy.

Laurel turned back to her patient, straightening the covers around his legs. "I'm afraid that leaves me out, then," she admitted ruefully. "I don't know much about cars. I just came in to make certain you were doing okay, and that Mrs. Gonzales didn't upset you too much."

"Gonzales?" The older man picked up on the name. "Isn't that the... wait a minute. He's the guy that got hit by the car."

Laurel shot another glance at Cade. "That's right." Her tone was hesitant.

"I recall hearing about that. That was a real shame. And you said he didn't make it?"

"No, sir. Unfortunately, he didn't."

"I hope they find who did it," the older man said. "That's just not right, hitting a fellow and then just driving off like that."

Clearly, Mr. Miller had no recollection of events immediately preceding his heart attack. Laurel knew that temporary memory loss wasn't unusual after any traumatic event, yet he remembered events of the weekend, namely the fact that Mr. G was the victim of a hit and run. Obviously, the detective wouldn't get a clear answer from the older man anytime soon.

Having come to the same conclusion, Cade stood and extended his hand. "Mr. Miller, it's been a pleasure speaking with you. I'll stop by and take a look at that car sometime. Sounds like a real treasure."

Wally Miller returned the shake with gusto, a big smile stretched across his wrinkled face. "Oh, she is, she is. You come by anytime, young man. Enjoyed visiting with you."

Cade followed Laurel out to the corridor, where he stuffed his notepad in his jacket pocket and released a weary sigh. "What do you make of that?" he asked, tilting his blond head toward the room behind them.

"I've seen it before," Laurel allowed. "After a traumatic event—especially where an interruption of blood flow and oxygen to the brain is involved—it's not unusual for a patient to experience memory loss."

"Temporary or permanent?"

"Honestly, it could be either. Only time will tell."

Cade gazed at the closed door with a thoughtful expression. "He certainly seemed sincere. I don't think he remembered a thing about his car being involved."

"Wait. You think that was all an *act*?"

"No," Cade said slowly, bringing that dark gaze to settle upon her, "I'm saying I *don't* think it's an act."

"But you still consider it a possibility," she pointed out, her feathers beginning to ruffle.

"I have to consider all possibilities, Nurse Benson." Whenever they were at odds, she noticed he referred to her in an official capacity. "In case you missed the news, forensics confirmed Mr. Miller's car was involved in the accident. We didn't release his name, just the fact that the car has been located."

"But you still think he may have been driving it." She made it an accusation.

"I certainly haven't ruled out the possibility. I have no proof that someone other than Mr. Miller drove that car last. Unless forensics finds that proof, or an eyewitness comes forward who can put someone other than Mr. Miller in the driver's seat, I'm afraid he remains our primary suspect."

Laurel was emphatic. Propping her hands upon her hips, she insisted, "He is not faking that in there. He was truly appalled that someone could drive away from a hit and run."

"I agree. That's why I didn't press him on the issue and made it a friendly discussion about cars. But you have to know that at some point, whether he remembers reporting the damage or not, I *will* address the situation." His words were firm, making his position on the topic clear. His tone softened as he added, "I'm not totally insensitive, Laurel. I'll give him a couple of days to recuperate, but then I must question him about the accident."

"I still don't think he did it."

"As you've made perfectly clear." His tone sounded weary.

"Because you keep insisting otherwise!"

"I'm insisting on finding the truth. Is that so terrible?"

"It is if you railroad that poor man into possible murder charges!"

"Involuntary vehicular manslaughter would be more appropriate," he corrected.

"Which would still blame him for the death. And he would lose his license." Sympathy flooded through her, fueling her ire at the detective. She jabbed a finger into his chest to make her objections clear. "Maybe even his freedom, if they gave him jail time."

"That's not my call to make." Unlike hers, his voice remained calm. "As for his license, if the man can't see and/or can't remember something as significant as hitting another human being, then taking away his right to drive is the best thing I can do for everyone involved. I could be saving countless lives, including his own."

Only after making his statement did he reach up to remove her finger from his chest. He did so in a manner that wrapped his long fingers around her hand and gently pulled it away. He held it for a moment, his touch sending tingles of awareness racing up her arm.

"I'm not the enemy, Laurel," he said softly, leaning in toward her. His dark eyes were warm and insistent, urging her to understand his position.

"Neither is Mr. Miller," she whispered. Her voice lacked conviction as she stared up at him, mesmerized by his brown gaze and his electrifying touch.

After a long, energy-charged moment that zigged and zapped between them, a smile lifted one side of the detective's face. "Do you go to battle for all your patients like this?"

"Absolutely."

With what could have been the slightest of caresses, he released her hand and pulled away. "I admire your passion for your patients," Cade told her frankly. "I have a similar passion for the law."

It was Laurel's turn to offer a half-smile. "Is that your way of saying you aren't giving up?"

"Raul Gonzales didn't deserve what happened to him. You saw Mrs. G's reaction to his death. How could I give up? Don't they deserve justice?"

"Yes, of course. But…" With a frustrated sigh, she didn't even try to finish.

"Like yours, my job isn't always easy."

"I'm just asking you to keep an open mind. Being old and not being able to remember things two days after having a heart attack doesn't mean he's guilty, even if his car did hit Mr. Gonzales. It could have happened as he claimed. Someone could have stolen his car and taken it for a joy ride."

Cade's look was skeptical. "And returned it to the place they stole it from?"

"Why not? They could walk away as easily as they walked up, and no one would be the wiser."

"We're asking around," he assured her, "seeing if neighbors noticed anyone suspicious that day."

"Good." Because she wasn't sure what else to say—and because she wasn't ready for their encounter to end—Laurel's nod lasted longer than the situation called for. Rather lamely, she repeated, "That's good."

After an awkward moment, Cade shifted on his feet. It was clear that neither wanted to say goodbye. "I suppose I should let you get back to work."

"Yeah. And I guess you have more leads to chase down."

"I'm afraid there aren't many for this case," he admitted. Cade took the first reluctant steps toward the front. "I guess I'll see you when I come back to question Mr. Miller?" He made it a question, and a hopeful one, at that.

"Yeah, probably so." She offered a shy smile. "Bye."

Laurel was headed opposite him, further down the hall. She took only a step away before she turned back.

"Oh. I, uh, had lunch yesterday at Mama G's. Downtown, where the accident happened," she clarified. "One of the servers told me she saw it happen. Not exactly happen, I guess, but she saw the car. I think her name was Delores. I suppose you've spoken to her?"

Cade smiled, but an edge had slipped into his voice. "Doing my job for me now, Nurse Benson?"

Nurse Benson. The title effectively put the brakes on her thundering pulse and whatever silly fantasies were spinning in her head. She immediately went back on the defensive. With an artificial smile, she all but gushed, "Why, bless your heart, I wouldn't dream of it." Turning on her heels, she was already fuming.

There we were, having what I thought was a "moment," and then he has to go and get all holier than thou on me! she fumed. *Who does he think he is, acting like I'm some amateur sleuth, sticking my nose in where it doesn't belong? I'm just trying—*

"Laurel?"

His voice broke into her silent tirade. Turning back to look at him, she wished for the hundredth time that he weren't so good looking. He would be so much easier to ignore that way.

"Yes?" Her voice was terse.

"When I come back, maybe I could buy you a cup of

coffee."

Say no. It's probably just some ploy to get on your good side, so you won't object to him badgering your patients. Remember the plan to run, run, fast as you can.

But when she opened her mouth, the strangest thing happened. Instead of saying no, she heard her voice say with a hint of a smile, "Coffee sounds good."

CHAPTER EIGHT

Before leaving for the day, Laurel made a final round to check on patients. She spared extra time with the two patients who seemed to be there alone. She hadn't seen signs of visitors to either of their rooms.

Because she didn't consider Cade a visitor, Mr. Miller was included as one of those two. She made him the same offer she had issued Mrs. Lewinsky.

"Is there anyone I can call for you? Do you have anything that needs tending at home? A pet that needs checking, maybe?"

"No pets. But I do have a small fall garden," the old man mentioned. "I reckon I could get my neighbor to check on it for me. He can keep whatever he harvests for his troubles."

"I'll be happy to call him, if you'll give me his number."

"Sure. It's...." He paused, scrunching his face in thought. "Uhm, it's..."

Seeing he was having trouble remembering the number off hand, she smiled to put him at ease. "Just give me his name and the street, and I'll look him up in the phone book. Does he need to bring you anything from your house?"

"My slippers would be nice. These floors are mighty cold, even with these socks you put on me. And my own pajamas would be better than this contraption." He plucked at the cotton hospital gown as he rattled off his neighbor's name and address.

"No problem. I'll call before I leave for the night. Be sure and let the night shift know if you need anything."

Once back at the nurse's station, Laurel looked up the number and made the call, relaying Mr. Miller's request.

"I'll bring the clothes, but the garden is another matter," the neighbor said. "Wally hasn't grown a garden in close to five years!"

"Oh, dear," she murmured. "He does seem to be having a bit of an issue with his memory since his heart attack."

"That's nothing new!" the neighbor harrumphed. "Last week, he asked me and Martha to come over to dinner."

"I take it dinner didn't go so well?" she guessed.

"Besides the fact that Wally don't cook, the real issue is that Martha died four years ago. Wally was a pallbearer."

"So, you're saying his memory has been failing for a while now," Laurel surmised.

"Happens to the best of us," the neighbor said. "I know where he keeps the key. I'll fetch his clothes and be down in the morning, if that's not too late. Like Wally, I don't like to drive after dark."

Laurel couldn't resist. "Oh, so Mr. Miller still drives?" she inquired innocently.

"Just local. Mostly to Whataburger, doctor's office, and Wal-Mart. If you can't buy it at Super Wal-Mart, we figure we don't need it too bad."

"Would you say he's a good driver?"

"Sure. Always drives real slow and steady. Takes excellent care of that car, too. It belonged to his wife, so it has emotional value. He'd be devastated if something happened to it. I reckon he must have driven himself to the hospital, because it's not in his driveway. Although I keep telling him, the way he leaves it unlocked and all, someone's gonna steal it one day."

"He doesn't keep it locked?"

"Says he's lived on this street for forty-seven years, and never had as much as someone trespass across his grass. Claims if he can't trust his neighbors, the world's in worse shape than he figured."

"He has a point, but it's not just neighbors he should worry about. You never know about strangers."

"You're preaching to the choir, little lady. But try telling that to Wally."

After the briefest of hesitation, Laurel picked up her phone and braved a text to Detective Resnick. His number was already programmed in her phone. *Purely a precaution*, she had told herself when she saved it, *if an emergency arose.*

Did you know Mr. Miller leaves his car unlocked?

A few moments elapsed before she saw the bubbles, indicating he typed a reply.

Is this the lovely Nancy Drew?

If not for the lovely part, she would have taken offense. She suspected he knew as much. She fought a smile as she typed back.

Bless your heart, you ARE quite the detective!

Because he had also saved her number in his phone, it hadn't required any real sleuthing skills on his part. Not that he had to share that fact with her.

I do my best. But your tip is duly noted. Thanks.

She wasn't sure what they were doing could be classified as flirting, but whatever it was, it felt good. As maddening as the detective could be, there was no denying her attraction to him. There was something about him that she found charming, and she hadn't been charmed by a man since Kenton. Even though her flirting skills were rusty, she was ready to try them out again.

Maybe you could spring for a cookie to go with that coffee.

By the time she felt her phone buzz with another message, she was already clocked out and in her car.

Don't press your luck, Nancy. I'll keep you posted.

"Posted?" She read in disbelief. "Posted? What is this, some police bulletin? I swear, that man sends more mixed signals than a hay-wire traffic light!" She spoke aloud in the car, irritated with him once again. "The Nancy part sounds like he's flirting, but the posted part could have been a smile, could have been a frown. Just like today. One minute he's leaning in, lingering like he doesn't want to leave. The next he's all starch and shine again, back to his 'Nurse Benson.'" She did her best rendition of his deep voice as she pulled out of the parking lot, adding an extra dose of sass. "Brown eyes and tingles or not, I'm not sure he's worth all the trouble. Hot and cold. Up and down. Maybe I'm just lonely. I could think about getting a puppy. They have gorgeous brown eyes, too, and are probably less trouble than that man would be." She continued muttering to herself on the drive home, exploring the merits of adopting a pet.

By the time she reached home, she had talked herself

out of a puppy.

Now to talk herself out of thinking about the detective….

After a load of laundry and a late dinner, Laurel watched the news. Once again, Raul Gonzales made the top of the newscast. Funeral arrangements were pending, but all three restaurant locations would be open for business and accepting donations to fund a culinary scholarship set up in his honor. Even though the car that hit the businessman had been found, police were still asking witnesses to come forward. No arrests had been made yet and no persons of interest had been named, including the owner of the vehicle.

After the weather, Laurel heard her phone buzz with another message. Her heart skipped a beat when she saw Cade's number.

You still up?

Part of her wanted to play it cool and ignore the message. The part of her that felt like a silly schoolgirl with a crush grabbed her phone and replied.

For a little while. Gotta work tomorrow.

He didn't take long to reply.

FYI. Your tip may be worth two cookies on our coffee date.

Laurel wasn't sure what pleased her more—the fact that he took her tip seriously, or that he considered their coffee a date. Both had her smiling.

Oh?

Pleased or not, she couldn't sound too eager. Luckily, the lack-luster reply didn't deter him from offering more.

One for each sketchy-looking teen, seen lurking in neighborhood Sat.

Smiling, Laurel wrote back.

Lurking, huh?

From Cade:

Look it up in your handy Nancy Drew Dictionary. Should be under Suspicious Suspects.

Laurel couldn't resist taking a jab at him, even though she suspected it fell outside the scope of flirting. Maybe she was rustier than she feared.

In my edition, it's under More Viable Suspects than Nice Old Men.

She breathed a sigh of relief when he came back with an immediate reply. At least she hadn't completely alienated him.

You're using the outdated version.

Encouraged, she replied:

No matter. Good to see our tax dollars at work.

There was a slight lag in his next text, leaving her to wonder if he were as rusty as she was.

I guess I should say goodnight. We both have work tomorrow.

Laurel's fingers caressed the keys as she typed:

Night, then. Have a good day tomorrow.

Her smile was practically giddy when she read his parting words.

Sweet dreams, lovely Laurel.

After a long day at work, Laurel decided to treat herself to dinner out. She had been craving fish tacos since eating them on Monday, and even though one or both of *Mama G*'s other restaurants were closer, she found herself driving to the downtown location. She reasoned that while in the neighborhood, she could drive by Mr. Miller's house and make certain everything looked in order. She could carve out a few minutes the next day to go upstairs and give him a report, even though his friend, no doubt, was keeping an eye on things in his absence.

She found the house easily enough, a modest, well-kept home in an older neighborhood. The house lacked the charm of her own craftsmen, but the simple style fit the trend of the time. His grass needed trimming, but otherwise, nothing looked amiss. She couldn't help but note that his carport, minus the Monte Carlo, was open on three of the four sides, making it easy for someone to come and go as they pleased. Only a small window on that end of the house overlooked the carport, so she could understand how Mr. Miller might not have known the car was ever missing.

As she drove the three blocks to the restaurant, she considered scenarios of what might have happened.

A couple of bored teens, looking for something to do on a Saturday afternoon. On a whim, perhaps, they decided to see if any of the neighborhood cars were unlocked. They hit pay dirt under the Miller carport. It should have been easy enough to hot-wire the '75 model. That was long before keys with chips and the new generation of anti-theft mechanisms came along. Taking the classic out for a spin, they thought cutting wheelies in the parking lot sounded fun. A miscalculation on the car's wide swing...a toe too heavy on the petal...an unexpected pedestrian... It could have happened that way, right? They could have panicked, quickly returned the car where they took it from, and took off on foot.

It sounded plausible in her head.

Or maybe they were doing a gang initiation. Like it or not, we do have gangs in BCS, and the more the cities grow, the bigger the crime element grows, as well. Maybe the test was to steal a car, and the rest was a terrible accident. Or maybe—if that Icepick guy is any indication—maybe the test was something more sinister. Maybe the goal was to take someone out, and Mr. G was in the wrong place at the wrong time. Maybe they stole the car to avoid getting caught, and poor Mr. Miller was another unfortunate pawn in their sick game, same as Mr. G. Not something I like to think about, especially here in our nice little town, but it does happen. I hear about it on the news and see it on TV all the time.

She ran the idea through her mind, but quickly replaced it with another. She didn't like the thought of gangs and deliberating killings.

Maybe it's not something nearly so bad. Maybe the boys weren't really lurking. Maybe they were nervous because one of them had to be at work and knew he would lose his job if he were late again. His buddy just wanted to help him out and give him a ride. He thought he could borrow the car for a few minutes, take his friend to work, and return it with no one being the wiser. They took a short cut through Mama G's parking lot and things quickly went downhill. Maybe they were texting and driving, or arguing over the quickest route to get there. Maybe it was just one terrible mistake after another, and then they panicked and ran away, instead of offering to help. Yeah, that could have been what happened.

It was better than the last scenario that wafted through her imagination.

According to the neighbor, Mr. Miller was having trouble with his memory, even before the heart attack. But surely, he's not that senile yet! Dementia can do terrible things to the mind, but to completely block out something like that? Could he have been driving and then completely forgotten about it the next day? But, I can't imagine him just coming home and turning on the television like nothing was wrong. Even if he hit him, then panicked and drove off, to forget something like that three blocks later… No, I can't think that. Even if Cade asks, I don't think I'll tell him what the neighbor said. I've been known to forget plenty of things, myself, and I'm fifty years younger than Mr. Miller! If Mr. Miller was driving the car at the time of the accident—and I'm not at all convinced he was—then I'm sure he had no idea he hit a person. He may have thought it was a post, yes, but not a person. There's no way that sweet old man would have been able to drive away, had he known the truth.

Laurel chose to ignore the fact that, for the last scenario to work, his eyesight would have to be no better than legally blind, in which case he would still lose his license.

Leaving it all behind her, she stepped into the restaurant and inhaled a deep breath of its mouth-watering aromas. As she placed her order at the counter, she noticed the atmosphere in the room was much more sedate and somber than the first time she visited. It had much to do with the black ribbon on the door and the huge poster of Raul Gonzales. It sat on a card table, surrounded by prayer candles and offerings of condolence from his adorning patrons. Cards, flowers, and other small gifts cluttered the tabletop, along with a steel moneybox with a slit cut into its lid. Laurel couldn't help but notice that the box was chained to the table to deter theft.

A sweeping glance over the restaurant revealed that all of the tables along the back wall were taken. As she turned back to search for an available seat nearer the front, she heard her name called. To her surprise, Cade sat in the very booth she had occupied on Monday and was waving her back.

"I didn't see you there," she said. "Of course, I also wasn't expecting you here. Do you come here often?"

"First time as a customer," he admitted. He motioned to the empty seat across from him. "Have a seat."

"I don't want to disturb you. It looks like you're here on a date?" She eyed the extra plate of enchiladas beside his taco dinner. She tried not to think about the woman who occupied the seat next to him, even though the spot was currently vacant.

"Nah, these are mine." At her raised eyebrows, he confessed, "I couldn't decide between tacos or enchiladas, and, as usual, I missed lunch. I'm hungry, and the guy at the register said both were highly rated, so I decided to find out for myself."

"Good luck eating all that!" she laughed.

"Unless you're meeting someone for dinner, join me," he encouraged, biting into a chip. "My food just arrived, so you won't be far behind."

"Okay," she agreed with a shy smile. "But, please. Don't wait on me. Eat while yours is hot."

He flashed a disarming grin. "I was hoping you'd say that. I'm starved!" He picked up a taco and devoured half in a single bite. "Breakfast was a long time ago."

"By all means." She laughed again, amused by his ferocious appetite. "Busy day, I take it?"

He nodded as he polished off the taco. "Very."

"Any breaks in the case?"

"I know you mean the Gonzales case, but unfortunately, it's not the only one I have. Here, have some chips and salsa."

"At the risk of sounding like Nancy Drew—" she continued, even though a mischievous light twinkled in his eyes "—I've been thinking. I have a possible scenario to run by you." She recited the first scenario as she had imagined it. Two teens, out for a joy ride in a car that didn't turn as easily as they expected. She had learned to drive in her mother's Grand Prix, which couldn't turn on anything remotely resembling a dime. It took at least a half dollar.

Swallowing a mouthful of Spanish rice, Cade quickly shot down her theory. "Game Day, remember? Even the back parking lot was full."

"Oh. Okay, well, what if someone was taking a

shortcut through the parking lot, trying to save time? Got distracted for whatever reason—probably texting while driving—and didn't see him until it was too late?" She didn't go through the whole set-up of a friend helping a friend. No doubt, he would think it too sappy.

Instead of instantly negating her suggestion, Cade stared thoughtfully out the window. Even with moderate lighting, darkness enveloped the parking lot, particularly the area around the back door. He studied the scene of the crime as he chewed an enchilada from the second plate.

"That's something I'm having trouble with," he said, using his fork to point. "See how narrow that space is between the railing and the first parking space? Why would someone deliberately drive through there? There wasn't enough room to get through. Not only did they plow down Mr. G and the railing, they took off the front fender of his car. I'm having trouble imagining that anyone, even someone half blind, would attempt such a tight squeeze."

"So, what are you saying? You think this was *deliberate*?" She dropped her voice, so that when she squeaked out the question, no one else could hear.

"It's a theory I'm exploring."

Laurel's fish tacos were delivered, but she gave them only a cursory glance after the server left. "Why would someone want to hurt Mr. G?"

"Now if I knew that," he drawled, bringing his eyes back to hers, "I'd have the case tied up all nice and tidy."

"But… for all appearances, everyone loved Mr. G." She motioned to the card table and its overflowing bounty. As if on cue, a small maraca placed near the edge rolled and tumbled onto the floor.

"Appearances," he told her quietly, his dark eyes

taking on a nefarious glow, "are often deceiving. Nancy Drew 101."

"Nursing 101, as well," she snapped.

At that, he chuckled. "Calm down, tiger. I meant no offense. But things aren't always what they appear."

"I know that." She released a weary sigh. "And I didn't mean to snap. I just… I don't like to think about there being such evil in world." She pushed a hand through her dark curls. "I *know* it, of course, but I don't like to think about it. Even when I see the results with my own eyes, day in and day out, working in the ER as I do."

"I understand that," he said slowly. For a moment, his big hand covered hers across the table. "But I don't have the luxury of ignoring the possibility that this could have been intentional. I owe that much to Mr. Gonzales."

Before Laurel could add "And his widow," a loud crash sounded from the kitchen. Amid a clatter of dishes and a flurry of voices, Esmeralda Gonzales' voice rose loud and clear above the rest. In a heated mix of English and Spanish, she berated the staff and threatened to fire them all. Laurel was thankful for her limited knowledge of the woman's native tongue, certain half the words weren't fit for the gutter.

"Ouch," Cade winced. "She doesn't mince her words."

"I'm glad I don't understand most of them."

"Allow me to blush on your behalf," he muttered. "I know all people react differently to grief, but that is extreme."

"It's not the first time I've heard her go off like that," Laurel admitted. "And I probably shouldn't repeat this, but… one of the servers told me she had been like a rock through this whole ordeal, and not in a good way.

She used the words 'hard and cold.'"

In reply, Cade merely grunted. Tuning the rantings out, he turned his attention back to his plate. "You'd better eat, before yours gets cold." He repeated the same advice she had given him.

"I've been thinking about these all week," she admitted, diving into the offering on her plate. One bite, and she closed her eyes and hummed with appreciation. "Mmm. Yes. Everything I remembered."

"Like me and your avocado shrimp dip. I don't suppose you plan on bringing that again anytime soon?" he asked with a hopeful smile. It looked utterly breathtaking on him.

"I'll let you know if I do," she promised.

They chose to ignore the last strands of Mama G's rant, as they turned the topic to lighter subjects. After running through their impressions of the food and the restaurant overall, they touched on the busy day at their prospective jobs. As Laurel pushed away her plate and Cade still worked on his, they broached the subject at the forefront of both their minds.

"So, no Mr. Benson, I take it?"

"Nope. And no Mrs. Resnick?"

"Never even came close." He sounded almost proud of the fact.

"I came close," she admitted.

"What happened, if you don't mind me asking?" He paused in the act of biting into his final taco.

"Turns out, he was terrible at math."

He stared at her in surprise, going so far as to set his taco down and push the plate aside. "Let me get this straight. You ditched a guy because of his math skills?"

She nodded, her dark curls dancing around her face. "I thought he was 'The One.' He was a doctor at the hospital where I worked, and we had so much in common. We just clicked, you know? And he said I was The One, too. The trouble is, he also told that to a doctor down in Galveston. And to one of our anesthesiologists. And to his upstairs neighbor." Laurel shrugged, surprised to find that it no longer hurt so much to talk about. "Like I said, he was terrible at math. He couldn't grasp the simple concept of *one*."

"I can see where that could be a problem," Cade agreed, a smile edging his mouth. "I know I promised cookies, but I see they have *sopapillas* on the menu. Wanna split an order?"

"Are you kidding? I'm stuffed! And I have no idea where you could possibly put another bite!" She touched her stomach in protest, noticing how he traced the movement with his very appreciative eyes. She glanced at her watch, surprised that it was already so late. "Wow. I had no idea it was this late. I really should be going."

He surveyed his own watch and sighed. "Right. I have another busy day lined up for tomorrow." He glanced around, finding that most of the other tables were now vacant. "I guess we clean our own tables?"

"I think so."

They stood and gathered their trash, depositing it in the bins near the door. As they stepped out into the night, Cade put his hand lightly upon her back. "I'll walk you to your car. Which one is it?"

She took out her key fob and clicked. The lights flashed on a sporty little Mazda.

"You really shouldn't do that, you know," he scolded. "It announces exactly where you're parked. And if you have the kind that unlocks as you approach, *please* tell me it only unlocks the driver's side door."

"I'm not sure," she admitted.

Cade groaned aloud. "That's just begging for trouble. Someone could easily slip into the passenger side and you would have no way to stop them. Promise me you'll go into your settings and change it. Tonight. Right now."

"I'm not even sure I know how," she murmured.

"I'll show you." He opened the door for her and ushered her inside, waiting until she was seated to kneel down beside her and check the settings on her dashboard. Laurel tried to follow the steps, but found she was easily distracted by his cologne and the sight of his very masculine hand, punching buttons in rapid succession. She finally gave up, enjoying his blond head being so close, even if she could only see the back of it.

"Okay," he said, turning unexpectedly to smile in triumph. He was disturbingly close. "Got it fixed."

"Th—Thank you," she stammered, blushing because she had been caught staring. *Not to mention fantasizing.*

For one glorious moment, she thought he might close the distance between them and kiss her. His eyes moved to her lips and lingered, but he kept at a safe, if not maddeningly near, distance.

"Well." He drew out the word, clearly not sure of his next move.

"Well," she whispered in reply.

Another moment stuttered between them, before he slowly pulled away and unfolded his long body. Instead of straightening to his full six feet plus, he stayed bent just a bit, so that he could see her face. "I enjoyed our dinner," he said.

"Me, too."

"Maybe we can do it again?"

Laurel hoped she remembered to smile. She barely remembered to breathe. "I'd like that."

"So I'll see you around?"

"Sure."

When he stood back and gave her room to breathe, she managed to have a coherent thought. Before putting the engine in reverse, she informed him, "You still owe me those cookies."

His smile was nothing less than charming. "I'm looking forward to it."

"Me, too. Good night."

"Drive safely. And lock your doors!" he called as he shut the door between them.

Laurel was still smiling as she drove away.

CHAPTER NINE

Laurel had Thursday and Friday off, but she was scheduled to work the weekend again.

The Aggie game was away this week, but it was still a busy day in ER. Late in her shift, the ambulance brought in a new patient with non-life-threatening injuries. From a distance, Laurel could see it was a young man with a bruised and battered face. A friend was already with him, hovering near his bedside in a frightened pose.

Hoping to put both at ease, Laurel put extra cheer into her voice as she greeted them. The friend turned at the sound of her approach.

"Lily?" she gasped. "Is that you?" Her eyes immediately went to the patient on the stretcher. "Harold!" she cried in alarm. "Harold, what happened?"

"I, uh, tripped." The boy managed to speak around a busted lip that was twice its normal size.

Laurel made a quick assessment of his injuries.

Face pale and swollen. Dried blood around his mouth and teeth. Left eye swollen shut. Deep scratch on his nose, blood seeping to the surface. Dark bruise encircling his throat, consistent with strangling. Numerous lacerations and bruising on both spindly arms and across his chest. Evidence of old bruising across his collarbone and sternum, more extensive that I glimpsed last week. Shirt ripped to shreds, exposing an almost emaciated body. Several of the cuts deep enough to require stitches.

"I've never seen this sort of damage from tripping." There was a quiet reprimand in Laurel's voice. "Please, Harold. I can't help you if you don't tell me the truth. Who did this to you?"

"He told you," Lily spoke up. She had on different clothes than when she came in a week ago, but Laurel imagined she still wore the same dirt and grime. Her slim frame was no larger than her son's. "He tripped."

"Lily, I can help you. You just have to trust me." Laurel beseeched her with her eyes.

"Ain't your problem," the other woman insisted. "The kid's clumsy." But she averted her eyes, refusing to meet Laurel's pleading gaze.

"Harold—"

"Like she said. Clumsy," the teen said, before he, too, turned his head away.

After a moment of looking helplessly between the two, Laurel shook off her emotions and set to work. She cloaked herself with an air of professionalism, even when inside, she wanted to cry. Clearly, the boy had been beaten and strangled. Tripping didn't cause damages like these, particularly around the neck.

She could no longer ignore the very real possibility of child abuse. As soon as she had Harold's wounds cleaned and tended, she would make a call to Child Protective Services. She was duty-bound to report any signs of abuse and neglect, no matter how badly she felt for those involved.

With neither mother nor child willing to provide further details about Harold's injuries, Laurel did the best she could. The doctor came in and ordered X-Rays and stitches, before leaving Laurel to carry out his orders.

"I think we have you patched up," Laurel finally reported. "The tech should be in shortly to take your picture."

"I don't like pictures," the teen said sullenly.

"That's okay," she smiled. "These are of your bones. Lily, can I have a word with you? And I'll see about getting you some coffee, or something to snack on while we wait for X-Ray. Harold, you know the drill. Press the button if you need anything."

Lily followed warily into the hall, where she faced Laurel with defiance.

"Lily, you know I have to report this," Laurel told the mother in a voice that was firm, yet gentle. "Unless you can tell me what happened, I have to treat this like an abuse case."

The woman bristled immediately. "Abuse? What are you talking about?"

"You know how this looks. Unexplained bruising and cuts to a major portion of his body. Most concerning are the bruises already forming around his throat, clearly in the image of a handprint. Someone tried to choke your son."

"He told you. He tripped. He grabbed his throat when he fell, but his grip was too tight."

Laurel gave her a hard, level stare. "You're really going with that story?"

"Of...Of course. It's the truth."

"Then you leave me with no choice but to call the authorities."

When Laurel would have turned away, Lily grabbed her arm. "No! No, you can't!"

Laurel looked down at the dirty hand that clung to her arm with surprising strength. “Move your hand from my arm, Lily. Right this minute.”

Hearing the quiet threat in her words, Lily dropped Laurel’s arm and began apologizing, followed by something near blubbering. “You can’t. He’s all I got left. They can’t take him, too.”

“Too? What about your other children?”

“They took ‘em while I was in the hospital. Everything I did, I did for them, and now the State says I’m an unfit mother! You can’t let them take Harold, too!”

“I want to help you, Lily, if you’ll just let me,” Laurel said softly. “But you must tell me the truth about what really happened to Harold.”

For a moment, Laurel thought the other woman might crack and confess to her what really happened. But her eyes wandered to a space behind Laurel, and suddenly, the woman froze. Paling visibly, Lily completely withdrew from Laurel, like a turtle retracting its body inside its protective shell. With a stubborn lift of her quivering chin, she avoided Laurel’s eyes as she said in a small voice, “I done told you. He tripped.”

Laurel shook her head sadly. “I’m sorry, Lily. I have to do this.”

Lily mumbled something as she turned away. Laurel thought it sounded like, “And I have to do this,” but she couldn’t be sure.

As Laurel turned toward the nurse’s station, she thought she caught a glimpse of movement down a restricted corner of the corridor. As no other personnel were around, she decided she was mistaken. She made it halfway to the desk when an alarm went off in Room 3, demanding immediate attention.

Ten minutes elapsed before she had the patient settled and she felt she could leave. Even though she didn't relish making the phone call about Harold, she knew she must. Protocol demanded she start with her own supervisor.

Hushed but heated words drew her attention from the end of the corridor. Seeing no one in the hall, she decided it came from around the corner. As she approached, she could hear some of the argument.

"You tell your boy, if he gonna be flashin' money around, he better flash it my way. The boss don't like waiting." The voice belonged to a man.

She recognized the woman's hissed voice as Lily's. "I told you! You'll get your money."

"You have it? Or did H-Man in there spend it all already?"

"I'm gettin' it!" she hurled in a hushed tone. "You have no idea what I had to do to get it, either."

"Don't know, don't care. Just want my money."

"I have till Tuesday."

"The date changed. You have till tomorrow."

"Tomorrow? Tomorrow!" she squeaked.

"Tomorrow. Twelve noon." The man's voice was cold and sharp. There was no denying the threat in his words. "Or I pay your son another visit. And this time, I won't be so gentle."

Before Laurel dared turn the corner, Lily came barreling around it, her face drained of all color. She brushed past Laurel without speaking, leaving the stunned nurse to sputter in surprise. By the time Laurel collected her senses and stepped into the adjoining hall, there was no sign of Lily's antagonizer, but she knew who it was. Icepick.

She followed Lily back to the room, where the

mother was sobbing quietly as she clung to Harold's hand.

"Lily." She spoke gently, so that she wouldn't startle the other woman.

Her head jerked up and Laurel saw that tears streaked her dirty face.

"What do you want?" she spat.

"I want to help. Please, let me get help for you and Harold."

"Too late. We're way past help," she said. There was a level of defeat in her voice Laurel had not heard before.

"It's never too late. Please, let me help."

"You can't. Don't you see? You can't!" The woman crumbled over her son's chest, sobbing onto his recently stitched wounds. Harold lay in the bed, his face stoically turned away to stare at the far wall, but tears leaked from his good eye and left tracks in his bloodied, dirtied face. The pair was a sad, pathetic sight, and Laurel's heart ached in empathy.

Laurel stepped forward and put a hand onto Lily's back, offering comfort. In the days since she had been admitted, the already too-thin woman had lost even more weight. Her body was even frailer now. Laurel had no problem feeling the bones that lay just beneath her skin and the layer of clothing.

After an initial stiffness, she felt Lily relax under her touch. But then Lily raised her head, and her eyes once again went beyond Laurel, to settle on a face in the hallway. Her own face closed down once again, and she flinched away from Laurel's hand.

"Get away from me," she said coldly. "Leave me and my son alone."

"I can't do that. He's my patient."

"I want a new nurse." Without warning, Lily began

screaming. "Doctor! Doctor! I want a new nurse! Get this one out of here!"

"Okay, Lily. Okay." Laurel backed away slowly, keeping her voice calm and her eyes on the frightened boy in the bed. He looked, suddenly, no bigger than a grade schooler, as his body curled in a defensive pose, shriveling before her very eyes. Broken hearted, Laurel continued to back out of the room, knowing she could do nothing more to help them. All she could do was get them help.

She bumped into another body as she backed into the hall. Expecting to see the nurse or doctor Lily had called for, Laurel whirled around, gasping when she recognized the man behind her. The diamond stud embedded in his tooth flashed with ominous sparkle as he offered her a leering smile.

"What are you doing back here?" she demanded. She was proud that her voice came out sounding strong and brave, when she felt anything but.

"Came to check on my boy," the man said, grinning as if he had no cares in the world. Up close, his tattoos were more graphic than she had realized. They were also more frightening.

"I'm afraid I'll have to ask you to leave. Only family is allowed with a patient."

"Hey, we all one big family." He leaned around to wink at Harold, who still shivered on the bed. "Ain't that right, H-Man?"

"*Immediate* family," Laurel amended. "Please, sir. You really must return to the waiting room."

"Sir, huh?" he grinned, the diamond flashing again. He stroked the skinny goatee on his chin, its dark hairs twisted and braided into a single strand. "I like that. In fact, I like *you*."

"That's good to know," she said, keeping her voice carefully neutral and her smile vague. "Then please help me out and let your friend get some rest. I'll let you know if he's accepting visitors later."

"You'll walk me out?"

Her hesitation was so slight, she hoped it went unnoticed. "Sure. Right this way, sir."

Icepick was slow to follow. Those few stalled steps allowed him to toss an icy glare into Harold's room. He made a motion with his fist, and Laurel shivered as she realized what it meant. It was a silent reminder of how he had gotten his nickname, and it didn't bode well for the vulnerable duo.

Her skin fairly crawling with disgust, Laurel did her best to keep a steady gait toward the front. What she really wanted to do was take off at a dead run, rushing the vile man out as quickly as possible. At the least, she wanted to put a wide chasm between them. Instead, she clicked along steadily, one hurried step at a time.

Icepick, however, had other plans. He ambled slowly toward the front, apparently pleased to have the pretty nurse by his side. He dragged his feet, forcing her to match his leisurely pace.

"No one ever told you to stop and smell the roses, girl?" he asked.

"I'm afraid that's a luxury I can't afford here in the ER. Every minute counts."

"I get it. I like knowing you're keeping an eye on my boy back there."

Laurel didn't point out the fact that Lily had kicked her out of the room and requested a new nurse. Undaunted by her silence, he pushed the conversation. "Yeah, we go way back. I don't want to see nothing bad happen to H-Man and his mama."

"Of course not," Laurel murmured.

"So, you be sure and relay a little story to him for me. A little reminder from me to keep his chin up."

Can you not walk any faster? I could walk backwards on my hands and still be there sooner! Come on; just pick your foot up, *instead of shuffling it. Hike up those baggy britches and walk!*

"You tell him," the man continued, unaware of Laurel's wandering mind, "one of my favorite bedtime stories. Be sure his mama hears it, so it can put her at ease, too. Tell him about the time someone gave me a canary in a pretty little cage."

Suddenly listening, Laurel looked at him in surprise. "A canary?"

"Oh, yes. A pretty little thing, too. So young and delicate. So helpless." His eyes glittered as he fell into story-telling mode, and his rough voice dropped to a quieter note. The drop, alone, sent a chill across her skin. "I kept it in its own cage, a nice shiny thing that kept it safe from all the big, bad cats in the neighborhood. Who knows what would have happened to my little canary, if I wasn't there to protect it?" If his smile was meant to be reassuring, it sadly missed its mark.

Laurel had a bad feeling about this story. She had a worse feeling about its storyteller.

"I had the bird for a long time. It was still such a pretty little thing, but it never did sing. And then—" he drew out the words as they finally neared the front of the long corridor "—one day—it did."

His feet stopped in the middle of the hall, as abruptly as his words ended. Laurel had to stop and look back at him.

"You know what?" he said, looking suddenly sheepish. "Maybe you shouldn't tell them that story, after all. I forgot. It has a sad ending."

Laurel refused to take the bait, but it didn't matter. He was determined to finish the thinly disguised threat. "H-Man and his mama might not rest well, when they hear what happened to my canary. You might not, either. You see, pretty and sweet as it was, when that little bird started singing, its *squeal* was so loud and so high-pitched, I couldn't take it no more. I had to silence it."

He leaned in close. Much too close for Laurel's comfort. She was certain he could hear the gallop of her heartbeat.

"Know what I did?" he asked in a conspiratorial tone, black eyes glittering. He made the motion with his fist again, a quick downward jab that sliced through air thick with tension. "Icepick. Straight to the heart."

He chuckled as he straightened and pulled away. "That's how I got the nickname. To this day, they still call me Icepick." His gaze flickered to her nametag. He curled his lip back, so that the diamond sparkled again as he offered what passed as a smile. "You have a nice evening, Nurse Benson. And have a safe drive home."

With knees weak and unsteady, Laurel watched him saunter through the door. She closed her eyes once he was gone, asking God for strength and protection. Even before he made his threat, she knew Icepick was a very dangerous man. She had hoped to avoid the man and remain forever anonymous to his world. But after that story, she knew she had unwittingly gotten his attention.

Cami St. John had taken Laurel's place in Harold's room. *Maybe it's for the best*, she decided. As usual, she had gotten too emotionally involved with her patients. Perhaps the best thing for Harold and his mother was for her to step back and allow someone else to take over. With her shift almost over anyway, Laurel finished up her charting and clocked out at one minute before seven.

As she drove home, she kept thinking about the thug called Icepick and the chilling story he had relayed. How had Lily gotten tangled up with such a man? Drugs, no doubt. At the very least, borrowing money from a known loan shark. Either way, she now owed him money, and he wanted it back. Apparently, Icepick's boss would stoop to any means to make his point, even roughing up a teenage boy.

"But didn't he say Harold was flashing money around town?" she asked aloud to the empty car. "That doesn't make sense. Where would he get money? Last week, he didn't even have enough to put in the vending machine. And would you *please* dim your lights and get off my tail!" This, to the unwitting car behind her. Naturally, the driver couldn't hear her, even though he or she practically hitched a ride on her bumper.

Have a safe drive home.

Icepick's parting words whispered through her mind, and she jerked her attention to the rearview mirror. How long had that car been following her? Had it been behind her since she left the hospital? Was it Icepick, there to reinforce his threat not to squeal?

Trying not to panic, Laurel spotted a drive-through restaurant ahead on her left. With little warning, she darted through traffic and pulled into line. Even though she had lost her appetite at the first sign of Icepick back in the ER, it gave her a few minutes to think. She wouldn't go home, not directly. She would take a winding route to her house and hopefully ditch whoever was following her.

If, in fact, someone did follow her. It could be her imagination, she reminded herself, heightened by Icepick's sinister method of telling a tale.

It took her twenty minutes to get home, even though

she lived less than ten minutes away.

Laurel was taking no chances.

CHAPTER TEN

Laurel was in for a long, restless night. Even for a Saturday night, there seemed to be more activity along her street than normal. Twice when she looked out, she imagined that the car driving past her house was creeping at a snail's pace.

She considered calling Cade, but told herself she was being ridiculous. There was no law against driving slowly down a residential street—just the opposite, in fact—even at one in the morning. Or at two, or even at three.

"Girlfriend, you look terrible," Danni told her with cheerful candor the next day.

"I didn't sleep well," Laurel grumbled.

"Detective Hot Stuff keep you out too late?" she teased.

"Hardly. There was just a lot of unusual traffic on our street last night."

"But you live on the most boring street in town!"

"Exactly. So even one car after midnight draws attention. Let alone three or so."

"Someone must have spiked their Geritol and thrown quite the party," Danni teased.

"Something like that," Laurel grunted. "I need more coffee. If we've got a spare IV pole, I may hook up to the coffee pot and pump it in intravenously."

Danni laughed as Laurel stumbled to the break room for her umpteenth cup of java this morning. So far, she was more jittery than she was alert.

Late in the morning, she was in for a rude awakening. Admissions brought back a walk-in patient, and the sight of the shaved head with a single Mohawk braid was like a splash of cold water to her senses. Icepick sauntered into the ER corridor, his sharp eyes searching for her. When he spotted her behind the desk, the diamond stud flashed and he pointed his finger directly at her.

"Her. I want her."

Unfortunately, he was on her side of the hall and Laurel couldn't gracefully get out of treating him. Not that she would have taken the coward's way out, even given the opportunity.

"So," she said in a firm, clear voice that held only the slightest of tremors. *Caused by caffeine*, she assured herself. "What brings you in today, Mr. —" she glanced down at his wristband "—Smith?"

Mohammad Smith. An alias, if I've ever heard one.

"I got a hurtin' in my gut. It's real bad."

"Hmm. Probably gas," she suggested.

"I don' think so. I got an iron stomach."

"Even iron rusts, Mr. Smith," she told him. "Open up." She jabbed the thermometer under his tongue and took no extra efforts when fastening the blood pressure cuff around his arm. She made certain it was tight, perhaps to tame the snakes whose images slithered up his sinewy arms. To be so skinny, the man had some serious muscle.

"Easy there, Nurse Benson," he said, but his eyes

danced with humor. "What's wrong? Didn't you sleep good last night?"

"I slept fine," she lied. "No talking while I take your vitals, please."

She left his room as quickly as possible, but he kept pressing the buzzer to call her back. His pillow needed fluffing. He thought he might be sick at his stomach. Was that a normal reading showing on the monitor? Could she bring him some ice chips? What did those new numbers mean?

Around the seventh call, Laurel decided to make him wait. He was across from the nurse's station, so he could see each time she sat down. Invariably, he chose that moment to press the call button. She tried sending Danni in her stead, but he insisted on having her as his nurse. Most often, he waited until she was the only one available to call for help. Eventually, Laurel simply looked up from her desk and made a visual assessment.

"Be right there," she would promise. Or, "Doctor's on his way back in." Once, when she took a seat and heard the familiar buzz coming from his room, she lifted a magazine and waved it in the air. "Sorry," she said. "Gotta brush up on my brain surgery technique. Doc says I may get to give it a try. Would you like to volunteer?"

Her answers amused him more often than not, something she hadn't intended. She was trying to thwart his attentions, not encourage them! She idly wondered if it were unethical to give him a double dose of unprescribed stool softener. *If his stomach hurts as badly as he claims, it may even help*, she rationalized.

As soon as she saw the physician attending *Mr. Smith* she asked in a hopeful voice, "Are we ready to cut the patient in Room 4 loose?"

"Not so quick. I'm not convinced of his pain, but his tox screen doesn't look too good. He's got some pretty wacky numbers going on. I want to run a couple of tests and get an X-Ray."

For a fleeting moment, Laurel felt a stab of guilt. Could it be that Icepick was truly sick? Had she allowed her personal dislike of the man to color her professional judgment?

Before she could feel too guilty, he pressed the call button again. She held back on the smart remarks and dutifully went into his room to assist him.

"Yes? What can I do for you?"

"What time is it, Nurse?"

"Almost noon." She pointed to the shiny gold Rolex on his wrist. "I've always wondered about those fancy watches. Let me guess. They look pretty, but don't work worth a dime."

He grinned, consulting the watch, which showed five minutes until the hour. "Just checking," he explained. "Didn't know if my watch would turn out to be like my canary. All pretty, no performance."

She refused to let the reference to last night's threat intimidate her. This morning, she was running on caffeine and not accepting any flack. "Well, if you end up stabbing the watch, remember to take it off your wrist first," she suggested dryly.

To her surprise, Icepick barked out a peal of laughter. "You alright, you know it? I like you."

"Can I do anything else for you?"

"It's almost noon," he repeated, watching her face for a reaction.

"Yes, that's correct."

"That don't mean nothing to you?" he questioned.

"If you're hinting for a tray, I'm afraid you're out of

luck. The doctor has called for more tests."

At mention of more tests, a wary look crossed his face. "What kind of tests?"

"I'm sure she'll be in shortly to explain it all. But until then, no tray for you, I'm afraid."

"I ain't hungry, anyway," he claimed.

"Then why all the questions about noon? If you're pointing out the fact that you've kept me from my own lunch, my stomach has already made that clear."

"You a spunky little thing, I give you that." He leaned back against the pillows, staring at her intently. "You really don't know who I am, do you?"

"Sure I do. You're Mohammad Smith."

"I'm the man who holds your friends' fates in his hands," he boasted, presenting both palms upward. "You might say that's their lifeline right there."

An uneasy feeling filtered through her, but Laurel refused to let it show. She bent over, pretending to search for the line. "And which friends are these?"

"H-Man and his mama. You heard what I told her."

She managed to look the man in the eyes, insisting with sincerity, "I really have no idea what you're talking about."

It was true. She vaguely recalled overhearing something about noon, but too much had happened since then, namely his story about the canary and a very sleepless night. And even if she remembered the conversation verbatim, she still didn't know the details. She could guess, but she didn't know.

Icepick stared at her for a long moment, but he finally grunted and broke his steady gaze. When he picked up his phone and tapped out a brief message, Laurel allowed her knees to sag. She hoped he hadn't noticed.

"You just bought your friend twenty-four hours. And

only because I like you. Tell her it's the last chance she gets."

"I think you have the wrong idea. I can't give her a message, because I have no idea of how to get in touch with her. I'd never seen either one of them before, until Lily walked in here last Saturday." She readjusted the cuff, making certain it was extra tight. "Come to think of it, she was complaining of a stomachache, same as you. Maybe she was contagious."

"You best pray her ailment ain't contagious. You wouldn't wish that on nobody." He followed her with his black, unreadable eyes. They were no longer laughing.

Showing the first sign that his threats affected her, Laurel's voice came out a bit breathless. "The doctor will be in shortly."

She walked from his room, directly into the break room. Despite her claims of being hungry, she had no appetite. And despite her show of bravado, she was trembling like a leaf, now that the confrontation was over.

After a moment's hesitation, she pulled out her phone and texted Cade.

I may have a problem. Are you anywhere near the hospital?

It seemed forever before she saw the bubbles of him typing.

I can be.

Relief flooded through her. She had been sorely tempted to call him last night, but she wasn't accustomed to running to a man to solve her troubles. Even when that man was a law officer.

Thanks.

Another slight delay before he replied.

Be there in 10.

As an afterthought, he added:

Hope there's room for a horse trailer.

She wondered what that last statement meant, but until she had at least one more cup of caffeine, she wasn't making any speculations. Knowing so much coffee on an empty stomach was a recipe for disaster, she found a stale croissant and popped it into her mouth. She finished it off as she walked back to her desk, still under Icepick's amused and ever-watchful stare. He seemed to keep an extra close eye on her, perhaps to see if she would contact Lily.

The trouble was, even if she wanted to pass on his message, she truly didn't know how to reach the other woman, short of calling her work. She imagined how that conversation might go. *Please tell your employee she doesn't have to leave town just yet. Her loan shark granted her an extra day.*

Wondering where such a cavalier attitude came from, Laurel reminded herself of the seriousness of the situation. This was hardly a laughing matter. Cade would—

Cade. How would Icepick respond to seeing the detective here? So far, she had managed to stay on the goon's good side (assuming he had one) but things might turn south if he thought she betrayed him. She picked up the phone to text Cade back, just as the front door binged and a new patient came in.

An odd jingling sound echoed along the hallways, drawing everyone's attention.

"Oh. My. Stars." Danni's mouth fell open as dropped back against her chair, her eyes enormous. "I've died and gone. To. Heaven. No doubt about it."

Even Laurel did a double take. Her mouth went dry when she saw Cade, tramping down the corridor in full cowboy attire. Her eyes started at his feet and traveled slowly upward.

Spurs jingled on the heels of his cowboy boots. Faded jeans hugged his long legs, covered in part by genuine rawhide chaps. A shiny belt buckle rode low on his flat waist, and sweat made his blue western shirt cling to his sculpted abs and chest. A bandanna knotted at his throat and a smudge of dirt marred one cheek. As he strode down the hall with a purposeful gait, he used one long finger to adjust his hat, pushing the gray felt brim upward so that it didn't interfere with his searching gaze.

When his eyes met hers, some of the tightness around his mouth relaxed.

Laurel glanced toward Icepick's room. He couldn't see who was in the hallway, but he watched their reactions with intense curiosity. If what he said was true and she had spared Lily and son certain grief, if only for one extra day, she didn't want to jeopardize their safety now. She needed to create a distraction.

Spotting a roll of gauze on the counter, Laurel grabbed it and hurried round the desk, flying toward Cade. Once she was past Icepick's line of vision, she made a 'shush' sign with her finger.

"Just go along," she whispered to Cade when she reached him. "I'll explain later." Tugging his left hand up, she began winding the gauze around it. "Play like it's cut."

To his credit, Cade went along with the crazy scheme without asking questions. By the time they walked past Room 4, he was nursing his hand, holding it close to his heart. Laurel stopped at the nurse's desk only long enough to tell Danni the same thing she had told the detective. "Play along. I promise to explain later."

Catching up with Cade, she used her instructional

voice as they continued past the room. She didn't dare look inside, but she could feel Icepick's eyes on her. "Try to keep your hand up, sir, so that it won't throb so badly. Above the heart is best."

"Sir, huh?" Cade murmured from the side of his mouth.

They turned and started toward the opposite hall, presenting their backs toward Icepick. Not taking any chances, Laurel kept her voice low. "Don't look now, but we have an audience. For all they know, you're just another patient."

His teasing response stunned her so badly, her steps faltered. "You wound me," he quipped, brown eyes dancing with mischief. "And here I thought something was starting to happen between us."

Recovering, Laurel shot back, "As long as the patient in Room 4 doesn't know about it, we're good."

"Who is it?"

"Your buddy Icepick. The trouble is, he somehow has the impression *I'm* his buddy now."

This time, Cade faltered. The steady knell of his cowboy heels against the tile stuttered, missing a beat. "Excuse me?" His voice sounded like thunder.

Motioning to the first room, Laurel's voice was loud enough to carry. "Right through here, sir. We'll get you settled and take a look at that hand." So that only Cade could hear, she dropped her voice and hissed, "Shh. Don't blow it."

"I may blow my top, if you don't explain yourself right now," he warned darkly, but he said the words quietly as he pushed past her toward the bed. He plopped down, using his peripheral vision to check visibility of the room across the way. Obviously, Laurel had chosen this placement on purpose. He couldn't see the whole room, but he could see enough. "How have you gotten yourself tangled up with a man like *that*?" He spat the word in contempt.

"Not by choice, I can assure you. Can you take those spurs off?" she asked, eying the shiny contraptions strapped around his boots.

"Not with my hand wrapped up like a mummy, I can't."

"Then just try not to poke a hole in the bed," she warned. She wrapped the blood pressure monitor around his forearm, trying not to admire the toned muscles beneath her hands. "We're going to make this look as legitimate as possible while you tell me why you're dressed like a cowboy."

"Because I *am* a cowboy," he informed her. "I've been roping, which I usually do on my weekends off."

"I guess that explains the need for horse trailer parking."

"Quit stalling," he hissed impatiently, "and tell me why that man is in that bed over there, throwing daggers at your back! That's not a friendly stare, by the way."

Laurel nibbled her lip. "He may think I called you and asked you to come here."

"You did."

"But I don't want *him* knowing that!"

"Tell me what's going on, Laurel," Cade all but growled.

Seeing the outrageous numbers on the blood pressure monitor, Laurel looked concerned. "You need to calm down. Seriously. Those numbers are sky high."

"Because you won't tell me what's going on!"

"Open up, stay quiet, and I'll tell you," she ordered, popping a thermometer into his mouth. He glared at her over the slender stick.

"What I didn't tell you last week—that day we saw Icepick in the hallway—was that he was here to talk to one of my patients. Except he wasn't just talking, he was threatening." She ignored the way Cade's eyes widened and continued, "Apparently, a woman named Lily Moses owes him, or at least his boss, some money. He gave her ten days to come up with the rest of it. Yesterday, Lily was back here at the hospital. This time, her teenage son Harold was the patient. Someone had obviously beaten him up. At first, I thought it might be an indication of child abuse, something I had wondered about previously. But then Icepick showed up here, and just seeing him was enough to send Harold into a fetal position. I overheard Icepick and Lily arguing, and he moved the deadline up, saying she had to have the money by noon today."

With every new detail, the storm clouds in Cade's eyes grew darker. The scowl on his forehead deepened and he clearly wanted to speak, but Laurel kept the thermometer shoved beneath his tongue, long after it beeped. It was the best way to keep him quiet.

"Seeing how frightened they both were of the man, I asked him to leave. I even walked him to the door, not trusting him to follow instructions. I have no idea how he got back here, in the first place. Anyway, he took the opportunity to tell me a story along the way. Of sorts." When she paused with a frown, Cade made a sound of objection deep in his throat. He motioned toward the thermometer, but she ignored him.

"The story was really more like a threat," she continued. "He—"

She should have known that admission would get a violent reaction from her 'patient.' Cade grabbed her wrist with his unbandaged right hand, pulling the offending thermometer from his mouth. "He *threatened* you?" he all but roared. His long legs were already swinging off the bed, ready to storm across the hall and confront the other man.

"Would you *please* calm down and just play your part?" she reprimanded. "And let me finish."

"Fine," he snapped. "Make it fast."

CHAPTER ELEVEN

Making certain to block Icepick's prying eyes, Laurel leaned over and pretended to examine Cade's hand. "It was a story about a canary," she explained. "It was young and pretty and the perfect pet, but it never made a sound. Until suddenly, one day out of the blue, it decided to 'sing'. Quote, unquote."

"Talk to the police," Cade translated tersely.

"Its *squeal*, pun intended, was so irritating that he had to get rid of it. According to Mr. Mohammad Smith over there—that's the name he used—that's how he got his nickname. An icepick to the heart silenced the bird, once and for all."

As the blood pressure cuff pumped again, Laurel took one look at the mounting numbers and warned, "If you blow up our machine, you *will* have to replace it."

"It's not what I do to the machine you should worry about. It's what I'm going to do to that man over there," he ground out.

"The story was intended for Lily and her son, but just so I understood it could easily apply to me, as well, he followed me home."

"What? And you didn't call me!"

Laurel sighed, admitting, "Okay, I don't know it for certain. I may have imagined the whole thing. But he told me to 'Have a safe drive home.' There was a car behind me, and by then I was so shaken up, I just sort of assumed it might be him. I think I lost it, but later, a car kept driving by my house. Very slowly, all night long."

"Same car?"

"It was dark, so I don't know. Again, I may have imagined the whole thing."

"But he shows up again today." His tone said he didn't believe it was a coincidence.

"Exactly. With a mysterious stomachache, same as Lily."

At that, Cade frowned. "Wait. How does that fit in? Why would she fake a stomachache to get into the ER? Do you know this woman?"

Laurel shook her head. "Never saw her before she checked in last Saturday. Remember the boy hanging around the Gonzales family upstairs? That was Harold."

To make his visit look authentic, Laurel made a show of searching through cabinets and gathering a few unneeded supplies. "I don't know whether it fits, or not," she said. She returned to his bedside and began cleaning his hand with betadine solution. At least it gave her the opportunity to hold his hand. The contact was comforting.

"Fake symptoms aside, Icepick insisted on me as his nurse. He's just about worn the buzzer out, requesting I come in every couple of minutes. Then he made a big deal about it being almost noon. I think it was just a ploy to feel me out—get that look off your face. I said feel me *out*, not feel me up!—to see if I had overheard his threat to Lily. Which I did, but I acted like I hadn't. He must have believed me, because he gave me his glowing seal of approval. Joy, joy," she added, rolling her eyes. "Most importantly, he sent a text message, apparently calling off his goons."

She paused again, considering what she had just said. "Wait. I thought *he* was the goon, working for some mysterious 'Mr. Big.' Maybe he's middle management, with peons working under him." She pursed her lips, pondering that thought for a moment before dismissing it with a shrug.

"At any rate, he told me to get a message to my friend Lily and tell her that, because he liked me, he was granting her an extra day. The thing is, I have no idea how to reach her, and I told him that. But he was all serious again. To be honest, there was a look in his eyes that sent a chill down my back and gave even my hair goosebumps. That's when I decided I should call you."

"A week too late," Cade muttered, "but better than never."

"That's what I thought," she replied smartly.

"Seriously, Laurel," he said in gentle reprimand. "You should have come to me sooner." His voice softened as he curled his fingers around her hand, taking care that the move could not be seen. He ran his fingertips along the palm of her hand in a gentle caress. "I'm glad you trusted me now. I promise. I'll do everything in my power to protect you."

Laurel luxuriated in the glow of his warm gaze for a long moment, loving the feel of his fingers against hers. But a long moment was all she could afford, without arousing suspicions. Breaking his hold, she gathered her supplies.

"I'll explain to Dr. Ainsley that you're undercover. She'll play along, I'm sure."

"As long as our act doesn't extend to needles."

"Why, Detective Resnick," she dared to tease, "are you afraid of needles?"

"Not afraid," he corrected. "Just not a fan."

"I'll be sure and mention it to the doctor," she promised. She moved to the doorway and issued the customary parting. "Press the button if you need anything. The doctor will be with you shortly."

As she suspected, Icepick's call button glowed before she took five steps away from Cade's room. In case she failed to see the light, he called from her as she approached, "Nurse! I need you, Nurse!"

She plastered on a smile as she entered his room. "What can I do for you, Mr. Smith?"

"What's wrong with him?" he bluntly asked, using his goatee-adorned chin to indicate the newest patient. She could hear the suspicion in his voice.

"The cowboy? You know I can't discuss other patients with you."

"You know who he is, right?"

Laurel looked back toward Cade, pretending to give the question serious thought. To his credit, Cade had his head tilted back against the pillow, his face pinched with pain—or worry—as his eyes anxiously scanned the area, seemingly taking in everything and nothing, all at once.

"You know, I thought he looked familiar," Laurel agreed. "He's a rodeo superstar, isn't he? Didn't he win the National Finals last year?"

Icepick looked offended by her question. "You asking me? Do I look like a rodeo fan to you?" he demanded.

"Hey, I like to watch the sport, but I don't own a cowboy hat, either," she replied.

He grunted at her glib answer, but he didn't give up. His eyes cut back to the room across the hall. "Looks like he did something to his hand. Cut it? Break it?"

"Something like that," she agreed vaguely. "What can I do for you, Mr. Smith? You pressed your call button, and I'm sure you didn't ask me in here to discuss the National Finals."

"When's the doctor coming back in? I got things to do today."

"I'm not sure, but I can go check."

She used the excuse to slip out of the room. She motioned for Danni to meet her at the end of the hall, well out of Icepick's audio and visual range. After a quick explanation about Cade being undercover, she found the doctor to repeat the same story. Both agreed to help, slipping notes and messages along to other personnel so that everyone was on the same page.

Laurel noticed that not a single woman had an issue with keeping Cade's cover, especially if it required making visits to his room. Every female technician on the floor rolled her cart to his bedside, no matter what her specialty might be. Lacerations didn't normally require X-Rays, but that didn't stop Tami and Helen from pretending to take them. Donna went through the motions of taking blood and Angelica dropped in to discuss diet and nutrition. By the time the weekend chaplain, a young female in her first year of hospital ministry, stopped in, Cade pressed the call button to summon Laurel.

Both Danni and Mary Ann came. Finally, Laurel's amused face popped into view.

"My, my," she teased, her hazel eyes twinkling. "Aren't we the popular one?"

"If the Gynecologist shows up," Cade warned darkly, "I'm out of here!"

Laurel laughed at his statement, until she realized how serious he was.

"I can't even keep an eye on the other room," he complained. "A different person parades through here every three minutes! I'm trying to make some phone calls and send a few texts, and I can't even do that."

"I'm sorry. They're just trying to help."

He didn't let it go so easily. Still glowering, he continued to grumble. "Do you badger all your patients like this? If you do all this over a cut, I can't imagine how you respond to a heart attack!"

"I think it's the spurs," she admitted. "Women tend to find them irresistible."

Cade rolled his eyes. The sentiment was heartfelt, but it also offered an opportunity to look across the hall. "Has he said anything else?" There was no need to clarify with a name.

"He thinks we all think you're a rodeo star, and we're making fools of ourselves over nothing. I may have pretended to start the rumor that you're famous. So far, he seems more amused than suspicious."

"I'm trying to find someone who can locate your friend Lily and make certain she's safe, but I haven't had any luck so far. She was evicted from her last known address. It's the same address her employer has on record, as well as the hospital. Any other ideas of how to find her?"

Laurel shook her head with a helpless shrug. "None at all."

"My buddy is coming up here to get the keys to my truck. My horse is still outside in the trailer. Can you ask the front to buzz him in when he gets here?"

"Sure. What's his name?"

"Shane Ebersole."

"No problem. By the way, how long are you intending on staying?"

His answer was direct. "Until he leaves or you leave, whichever comes first."

Laurel bristled. "If you're suggesting I need a babysitter—"

"I'm suggesting I'm not taking any chances, and neither should you. There will be a car patrolling your neighborhood tonight."

"But—"

He held up his unbandaged hand. "This is not up for discussion, Nurse Benson."

"Great. We're back to Nurse Benson again. You know what? You seem quite irritated. I think I'll talk to the doctor about getting you a shot to calm you down."

She picked up his file and pretended to scan over it. The paper should have been empty, but to her surprise, there were several notations by various contributors.

Seriously hot… Dreamiest brown eyes I've ever seen… Hot. Hot. Hot… Got MY blood pressure up… ICU for two, please… I prescribe a bottle of wine and a quiet evening at home. With me, of course… I'll sign up for private nurse duty!… Me, too!

Feeling irrationally grumpy, Laurel muttered, "Maybe I should sell chances to see who gets to do the honors. It would be a clear money maker." She snapped the file shut and shoved it back in place. "Speaking of badgering patients… have you harassed Mr. Miller lately?"

"I've had the weekend off, as you can see," he replied, shaking his leg to make the spurs jingle. "So, I'm a little behind on my badgering schedule. But don't worry. That will change first thing tomorrow morning."

Her grumpiness dissolved into worry. "They didn't find anything in his car?" Her voice sagged with disappointment. "I was hoping they would. Fingerprints on the steering wheel. A long blond hair, maybe. A candy wrapper with someone else's DNA on it. Something."

"Unless he comes up with an alibi, none of those things will definitively clear him. No one else can prove that he *wasn't* driving the car at the time of the accident."

"I suppose you checked traffic cameras?"

"No, it never occurred to us," Cade replied dryly.

"Okay, sorry. You don't have to get snippy."

"Look, I don't like it any more than you do. He seems like a nice old man. But I've spoken to his neighbors, his friends, *and* his doctors. All tell me that he has had increasing problems with his memory. And a psychologist tells me that it wouldn't be uncommon for someone—particularly someone in a compromised mental state such as dementia—to subconsciously block a traumatic event from their mind."

"So, what are you saying?"

"I'm saying it's much more likely that Mr. Miller accidentally hit Gonzales, panicked, drove home, and then blocked the event from his mind so completely that he was genuinely surprised when he saw the damage to his vehicle the next day. That scenario is much easier to imagine than the alternative, which would have someone stealing his car, hitting the victim either intentionally or accidentally, and then returning the car to his carport. All without anyone seeing them, I might add."

"But the two teenagers…" she reminded him.

"Could have simply been walking down the street."

Before Laurel could make a comeback, she heard a familiar jingle from the hallway.

"Hey," a deep voice said. "They told me it was okay to come back."

"Shane! You made it." Looking past a still-irritated Laurel, Cade smiled at the man who had walked up behind her. "Thanks for coming down."

"My pleasure." A dark-haired cowboy in garb similar to Cade's directed his smile toward Laurel. "I had no idea this is where all the pretty women hang out. I should visit the ER more often."

"I'm not sure I would suggest that," Laurel laughed. "At least not as a patient."

"Be careful. This one is a bit needle happy," Cade warned.

His friend pretended to shrink back. "Needles? I don't do needles."

Laurel put her hands on her hips and looked between the two men. "What is it with you cowboys and needles? You face raging bulls and bucking broncs, but shy away at a tiny sliver of steel."

"I don't know what lies this one has been telling you," the dark-haired man said, "but we don't do bulls and broncs, either. We do team roping. Much less dangerous." He presented a large hand. "Shane Ebersole."

"Laurel Benson. It's a pleasure to meet you."

"Believe me, the pleasure is mine. No wonder Cade plans to spend the entire afternoon here." He looked at his friend and grinned. "Is there room for me in that bed? I may decide to join you."

"Would you like a chair?" Laurel offered. "There should be one in here, anyway."

"That would be—"

"He's not staying!" Cade barked, interrupting Shane's acceptance. He wasn't thrilled with the easy smiles flowing between his friend and the nurse. He gave his buddy a pointed look. "The horse. Remember?"

Shane waved away the concern. "He's fine. I checked him on the way in."

"I'm working a case here, you know," Cade reminded him. "I'm not here for a social visit."

The three women approaching the room told a different tale. A pretty blond came from the left, carrying a brochure about the hospital. The other two came together, fighting back giggles as they crowded into the space.

"I thought you might like to know about all the services the hospital offers. My name is Jennifer, by the way," the blond said, leaning deep to hand over the brochure. Laurel recognized her as an aide from Admissions.

"I'm Gayle. We're from Housekeeping. Is everything okay with your room?" one of the other women asked.

"I can bring you another pillow, if you like," her friend offered. "Or a blanket. If anything needs cleaning, just let us know. Ask for Helena. That's me, by the way."

Shane was all smiles as he surveyed first the trio of visitors, and then his friend. "My. They are certainly friendly here, aren't they?"

"You have no idea," Cade murmured. "Thank you, ladies. All of you. But I think I'm good."

One smile from the cowboy went a long way. The women melted away, perfectly content to have seen the man who had the entire floor abuzz. And he had a good-looking friend, too! Laurel swore she heard the women giggling as they floated down the hall.

"He's working very hard," Laurel assured the dark-haired visitor, trying to keep the smile off her face.

Shane made no such attempt. "I see that," he said with a broad grin.

"Unfortunately, I, too, have work to do. Shane, it was nice meeting you. Cade…" Laurel looked at the man upon the bed, wondering why he looked so disgruntled.

They were still at odds where Mr. Miller was concerned, but he was voluntarily giving up a Sunday afternoon to watch over her. Unsure of what to say, she went with a simple, "You have the button."

CHAPTER TWELVE

By the time the doctor released Icepick, Laurel felt as if she had been through the wringer. The man continued to press his call button at regular intervals, if for no other reason than the fact that he could.

"Good news," she said as she entered Cade's room. "Your gig is up. Icepick went home."

"I saw that. However, there is one small problem."

"What's that?"

He gave a rueful smile. "I sent my truck home with Shane and Drake. I don't have a ride."

She looked at her watch. "I don't get off for another hour or so, but if you don't mind waiting, I can give you a lift."

"Only if we can stop for dinner on the way home. Unfortunately, there was no spicy avocado and shrimp dip today. No offense to the lovely Cheryl from nutrition—or was that Angelica?—but the menu has gone sharply downhill since last weekend."

"Everything pales in comparison to Game Day feasts," Laurel agreed with a laugh. "I'm too tired to cook, anyway. Icepick nearly ran me ragged today. I thought they'd never release him!"

"Why did they keep him so long, anyway? I thought he was faking it."

"Yes, and no. Some of the results came back questionable, especially under the context of his supposed 'symptoms.'" She used air quotes around the word. "It called for a full battery of tests."

"That's what he gets for wasting y'all's time."

"He'll also get a nice, fat bill," Laurel said with a gleeful smile. "It almost makes the blisters on my feet worth it."

"Speaking of which… If I have a bill for the day, I'm sure the department will cover it."

"I doubt they'll bill you, as we never needed the room. And on that note, there's no need for you to hang out in here any longer. You're free to get up and roam at will."

"I could stretch my legs." He moved off the bed eagerly, swinging his long legs with a jingle of the spurs. "I don't know how sick people do it."

"Well, to begin with, they're sick," she reminded him with a teasing smile. "They *need* to be in bed."

"But all day? I'd go crazy! Not to mention stiff." He stretched and pulled his long body in different directions, working out the stiffened muscles.

"You did go above and beyond today. I guess I can spring for dinner tonight," Laurel offered.

"I know we just ate there, but I have a craving for Mama G's again."

"I'll go for anything tonight. I'm that tired."

Less than thirty minutes later, Laurel's co-workers took pity on her and insisted that she leave early. It didn't hurt that she had a dinner date with the handsome man in spurs, even though she reminded them it was hardly a 'date.' But seeing the way Cade touched her back and ushered her out the door, Laurel seemed to be the only one who thought that way. Her friends were still abuzz with gossip and more than a touch of envy, long after they left.

"Good," Cade said as they collected their drinks and turned from the restaurant counter. "Our table's free."

Laurel made no comment as she led the way to the table by the windows, but she was secretly thrilled to have what he considered 'their table.'

But as they settled in, she saw the scowl on his handsome face. "You didn't have to buy dinner. It doesn't feel right, letting the lady pay."

"Don't tell me you're one those chauvinistic men who think he has to pay for everything!"

"It's called being a gentleman."

"It's called eighteenth century. This is almost 2020. You should start seeing things that way."

"Fine. But next time, I pay."

"Fine. But next time, we're going somewhere really expensive."

He surprised her with one of his charming smiles, leaving her to wonder if he had deliberately tricked her. "Absolutely."

Did he just ask me on a date? A true date? Laurel bit her lip, replaying the conversation in her head. It *sounded* like a dinner invitation.

Cade gazed out the window, seeming to study the cars pulling in and out of the parking lot. An hour before closing time, most were going out, but a lone vehicle pulled in and left the motor idling near the back door. Its lights cast a dim glow into the gathering darkness.

"Yes," he told her, his eyes still on the window. She realized then that he could see her reflection in the glass and wondered if he had read her mind.

He had. Turning back to face her quizzical look, his dark eyes met hers. "Yes. I just asked you out on a date."

A bit shyly, Laurel tucked a loose curl behind her ear. Her words were low, but he could still hear the pleased tone in her voice. "And I just said yes."

The server came with their food, and the next few awkward moments eased amid the task of eating.

"I can't believe I'm so hungry. I thought for sure Icepick had ruined my appetite," Laurel said, digging into another enchilada. As delicious as the fish tacos had been, tonight she was trying something new. It didn't disappoint.

"I scouted the parking lot for about twenty minutes before we left. I'm relatively certain he wasn't waiting for you to get off work."

"I think that's a fair bet," Laurel said, her eyes twinkling. "The doctor gave him a little extra something before he left. Sort of a 'farewell, don't come back' kind of gift, if you know what I mean."

"So, he'll be otherwise occupied this evening?" His own brown eyes shone with delight.

"And probably part of tomorrow," she predicted.

She liked the sound of Cade's laughter. It had a deep, solid ring to it.

"So, you're a team roper, huh?"

"Yep. Shane and I have been partners for about ten years now."

"I imagine by now, you have your routine down pat," she guessed.

"Pretty much. Trouble is, the calves usually have a routine of their own." His rueful smile was as charming as all his others were. Laurel asked more questions, genuinely interested in his answers, and in hearing the sound of his voice across the table. Unlike many of their conversations, this one flowed easily.

The sound of sharp voices from outside eventually drew their attention. Laurel looked around, spotting an older model car parked in the lot, its lights and motor still on.

"Hasn't that car been there for a while?" she asked.

"Yeah. I saw it pull up about the time they brought our food."

"And we're almost done."

"There were a couple of teenage boys inside. I think that's them, talking with someone in the doorway." Cade nodded to the figures half-hidden in the shadows.

"Sounds like they're arguing. Reminds me of the last time we were here, and Mama G threw a temper-tantrum."

"Come to think of it, that's sounds a little like her voice."

"Probably chewing out a couple of employees," Laurel predicted. "That first day after the accident, I heard her on the phone, complaining about some stupid boy who would be finished the next day. I suppose she was firing him, too."

"She was conducting business from the ICU waiting room?"

Laurel shrugged, searching for the right words. "I know it sounds a bit… cold. But it happens. Life goes on, even when your loved one is lying in a hospital bed, clinging to life. I've seen it too often to think it's not the harsh reality of life."

Cade narrowed his eyes, peering out into the darkness. "Have you heard any more about the Gonzales' pending divorce?"

"Just rumor and speculation. One of the nurses said

she had heard it was an ugly fight. They had agreed on splitting two of the restaurants down the middle, his and hers, but the third location was the main point of contention, and it was a big one. I heard negotiations weren't going well, but again, all of that is speculation."

"I guess that location was a real money maker." Seeing the look on her face through the window's reflection, Cade shifted his eyes back to hers. "What?"

"According to what I heard yesterday, the third location wasn't doing so well."

"They were fighting over who got *stuck* with it?" he guessed.

"Maybe," she said. "I hear it has all the bells and whistles. The latest and greatest of everything, located in a very expensive shopping center. This person told me that the rent, alone, is ridiculous."

"How reliable is the source?"

"This came from one of our techs. His wife, Glenda, works at the bank that holds the note on that particular restaurant. One of the conditions of the loan is that each of the Gonzaleses carry a very hefty life insurance policy."

"How hefty?"

"I may be speaking out of turn, but large enough that it pays the loan off in full, with some left over, if something should happen to either of them."

Of one accord, both their heads turned toward the parking lot, where the sounds of an argument were getting louder. One of the teens backed up, getting out of the way of the large woman who jabbed a finger into his chest and yelled at him in Spanish. Laurel recognized the leopard-skin tights. Esmeralda Gonzales.

"She sounds really angry."

"Especially for a woman who just got a free

restaurant," Cade murmured, his expression thoughtful.

Laurel gasped, jerking her gaze back to his face. "You're not thinking…"

"Probably what you're thinking," he confirmed.

"I'm thinking that she was running hot and cold. One minute she was all business, the next she was hysterical. In the ER, she railed against the injustice of it all, demanded action, threatened to sue, and then curled up beside him like a lost kitten. I hate to say it," Laurel said with a sheepish look, "but we call them wifezillas."

"Hardly the actions of a woman going through divorce, wouldn't you say?"

"Maybe. But sometimes, tragedy brings out the best in people."

"And sometimes, money brings out the worst."

They turned again to look at the threesome outside. One of the teens turned, just enough for Laurel to glimpse his face.

"Harold?" she gasped. "That's Harold!"

"The boy from the hospital? Icepick's Harold?" Cade's tone was sharp.

"Y—Yes."

"Does he work here? Does his mother?"

"Not that I know of. So why would he be here, having a heated argument with Mama G? It doesn't make sense."

"You wait here. I'll be right back." He was already moving away from the table before she could protest.

He returned a few minutes later. The argument still ensued.

"Could you hear what they were saying?" She instinctively knew he had gone to the back door to listen.

"Something about money. Mama G owes them for a job they did, and Harold and his friend were demanding that she pay them. The friend sounded desperate."

"I don't like the sound of this. It looks like the fight is escalating. Maybe you should—Oh. My. Word. That's not two teenage boys out there! That's—That's Harold and Lily! That other boy is his *mother*!"

"*That's* Lily? She looks like a kid in those jeans and hoodie."

"She has a slight build and is dreadfully skinny. So is Harold." Laurel stared at the two outside, trying to make sense of it all. A sick feeling formed in the pit of her stomach. "At…At the risk of having you call me Nancy Drew, I…I have another theory I'd like to run past you," she said, nervously licking her lips. Her eyes never left the scene in the parking lot.

"I'm listening."

"Hear me out, before you say I'm a terrible armchair detective."

"Just tell me your theory!" he said impatiently.

"What if…What if the two teens that were seen on Mr. Miller's street were really one teen and one skinny mother who looks like a teen from behind? What if it was Lily and Harold that day?"

"Obviously possible," he agreed, motioning to the duo outside.

"We know that Lily owes Icepick and his boss some money. It has to be a serious amount, if he's willing to beat up a kid for it. And I know how desperate she seemed, and how defeated. She sounded as if she had little hope for herself."

"I've seen it often enough."

"Scraping together that kind of money would probably mean doing something illegal."

"It usually does."

"They came in at the same time as Mr. Gonzales, and

right from the beginning, they seemed more interested in his condition than Lily's. Originally, I thought she was there for drugs. Then I suspected she might be running from an abusive home situation. She seemed oddly reluctant to leave, even with three other children at home."

"What are you saying?"

"Her symptoms were all over the place," Laurel continued, as if he hadn't interrupted. "Every time a test ruled out one possibility, she came up with another complaint. At one point, I suspected she was tampering with her monitor. That maybe some of the crazy readings were from Harold, not her. He had a red mark on his arm, consistent with a blood pressure cuff. Her numbers were erratic enough that the doctor finally admitted her for the night. At the time," she pointed out, "Mr. G was still alive."

"And Harold kept hanging around ICU," Cade recalled. "I suspected something was off, but I thought he was waiting for Mrs. Gonzales to leave her purse unattended, so that he could steal from her."

"It's not so unusual, people being fascinated by a morbid situation, especially teenagers. But Lily's interest in Mr. Gonzales seemed over the top. She even encouraged me to leave her and focus on him."

Cade ran the scenario through his head, nodding as the pieces fit together. "It makes sense. Lily was desperate for cash and Icepick was pressuring her for more. They could have stolen Mr. Miller's car, used it to hit Gonzales—"

"Harold had a bruise across his chest, like a seatbelt would make!" Laurel broke in, remembering the angry red mark.

"—and then returned it, just like you said. They could

have parked their own car anywhere, even here in the parking lot, and walked the few blocks to and from. That would have given them reason to come back here and see the outcome."

"And when he didn't die at the scene, they needed an excuse to get into the hospital," Laurel theorized. "Hence, Lily's 'terrible bad' stomach pain."

"And who else to make such a large cash payout, than the widow who inherits everything, including a brand-new, virtually *free* restaurant? I've been looking into their finances and some of the inconsistencies in Esmeralda Gonzales' statement. I have reason to believe she could have benefitted from his death, both financially and personally. Plus, she would have known her husband's schedule, therefore providing the precise time for them to drive through the parking lot."

"She probably paid them half upfront, half when they finished the job. I know Lily only paid Icepick half of what she owed him. The rest is due tomorrow at noon."

"I'm guessing that's what this fight is about. She's desperate for Mama G to pay up."

"One thing doesn't add up. Harold came into the ER yesterday, all beat up because he was seen flashing money around, and Icepick thought he should have been the first one paid. If Mama G hasn't paid them the rest of the money yet, where did that money came from?"

"Who knows? It could have been a last-minute drug deal, or maybe he fenced something. Lily may have kept some of the money back from the first payment. Or maybe Mama G paid them in full, and now they're being greedy, trying to blackmail her for more."

"Not a wise choice, since it would only implicate herself," Laurel pointed out.

"Desperate people don't always think rationally."

"And I definitely think Lily is desperate."

"I know she is." Cade jumped up from the table, his voice tight. "Call 9-1-1. Tell them you're with me and give them the location. Tell them I'm off-duty and need immediate backup."

"What's—What's going on?"

"Stay put," he warned. "Whatever you do, don't leave this table." He leaned low, so that only she could hear as he brushed the words against her ear, already halfway to the door. "Lily just pulled a gun!"

CHAPTER THIRTEEN

Cade moved carefully toward the back door, reaching into his boot to pull his off-duty weapon. The door was already cracked, so all he had to do was open it enough to slip through.

Simple enough, except the arguing trio stood only a few feet away. Nothing but a vine-covered trellis separated him from them.

With any luck, it was enough cover to conceal his movements. The glare from the porch light's bare bulb helped disguise the widening triangle of light spilling from the hallway as he inched the door open. He flattened himself as much as possible as he slid through the narrow opening.

"Let's talk about this," he heard Esmeralda say.

"I'm through talkin'!" Lily snapped.

"You can't just shoot me!"

"Wanna bet?"

"Then how would you get the rest of your money?" Cade had to hand it to Mama G. For a woman caught in the crosshairs of a gun, she was surprisingly rational.

"Then get it for me. Now. I'm tired of waiting and

all."

"I don't have that much in the register."

"Get the donation box."

"It's in the office. I'll have to go back in," Esmeralda pointed out.

"Do you think I'm stupid? You'll call the cops! Just wait. Let me think." Lily paced back and forth, trying to come up with an idea. Inspiration struck, and she turned with a smile. "Harold, go inside and get the box."

Cade scrambled for cover. A large trashcan was his only option, but shadows from the trellis shrouded it with secrecy. He crouched low behind the black vessel, his long legs cramped in the space.

He couldn't see what happened on the other side of the trellis, but Cade heard Mama G huff out an indignant protest as feet shuffled closer. His guess was that Harold brushing insolently against her when he passed. Cade could see the self-important smirk on the teen's face as he sauntered inside. The boy didn't see him there in the shadows now, but Cade feared it would be a different story when he came back out.

From inside, Laurel watched the scene as it played out. She made the call as Cade requested, giving the operator as much information as possible, but that was ages ago, or so it felt. What was taking so long?

He had told her to stay there, but Laurel didn't like being left out. After a moment's hesitation, she grabbed her purse and hurried around the corner and down the hall. The back door stood slightly ajar, but there was no sign of Cade.

She would just tiptoe to the edge and peek out…

There wasn't much to see from that angle, including anyone outside, but she could hear most of the conversation.

"You'll get your money, *mujercita*, just as soon as I do," Esmeralda promised.

"I can't wait that long! I need it now!"

"Waving a gun won't make it appear."

"No, but shooting you will make me feel better!" Lily screamed. "Do you know what we did for you? We got rid of your husband, just like you asked, but it cost me my kids! And now Harold's been beat up, because you won't give me the rest of my money!"

"You can have the donation box. There's a couple thousand dollars in there."

"You owe me more than that!"

"And I will pay you, *mujercita,* but not tonight."

"Quit calling me that! I don't even know what it means!" Laurel imagined that Lily put her hands to her ears, near her breaking point with the unfamiliar phrase and the stress of the situation. She could hear it in her voice.

Esmeralda must have heard it, too. Her own words became more hurried, her tone less relaxed. "Little woman," she assured her. "It means little woman. No disrespect."

She said something more, but Laurel missed it. There was movement in the hall behind her, and then she felt the edge of something cold and hard pressed against her back.

"You can't keep your nose out of things, can you?" a voice sneered.

"H—Harold? Is that you?" She started to turn around, but the cold metal jabbed into her with force. More surprised than hurt, she let out a small squeal.

"Don't turn around. I have a gun in your back. You're coming with me."

"Harold, what are you doing?" she cried.

"I said don't turn around! I'm not kidding, lady. Just do what I say. Go." Despite the harshness of his words, Laurel heard the way his voice trembled. He was as frightened and uncertain as she was.

"You don't have to do this, Harold," she said softly. "I told you and your mother I would help."

"You can't help. We've done too much. Just walk."

When he gave her a shove, Laurel stumbled through the doorway. She almost lost her balance and went down, but she caught herself just in time. As she righted herself, she saw Cade crouched behind a trashcan. Even in the shadows, she could see the rage that filled his face, and she knew that much of it was directed at her for not following orders.

Trying to throw Harold's attention the other direction, Laurel raised her hand and pointed to the parking lot. "Is that your mother out there?"

He sounded irritated, but his eyes apparently followed her movement. "Yes. Now walk."

When they stepped around the trellis and into Lily's view, his mother was clearly not pleased.

"Harold! What are you doing, bringing her into this?"

There was a whine in his voice as he answered. "She was poking around in the hall. She heard you, and she saw me with the money."

"What are we supposed to do with her now?" his mother asked, her eyes wide with horror. Her gun arm sagged. "I ain't killin' no one else."

Esmeralda took the words to heart and made a step backwards. Realizing her mistake, Lily brought the gun back up, waving it in the bigger woman's face. "Except you. I don't mind killing you, and all. You deserve it!"

"How do I deserve it?" Esmeralda was indignant. "I paid you good money to do the job!"

"But you only gave me half!" Lily screamed. "I need the rest!"

"I told you. Half before, half when the insurance pays."

Behind her, Harold nervously shifted from one leg to another. "What do we do with her?" he asked, shoving Laurel forward to stand beside Esmeralda. When he came around in front of them, taking his place at his mother's side, Laurel saw the only thing in his hand was a familiar-looking cash box.

I was held up by a cash box! She thought in dismay.

Lily looked from Laurel to Esmeralda. "How much did the other donation boxes bring in?" she demanded.

"About the same. Maybe two thousand each, give or take."

"We're going to take a ride," Lily decided. "All of us. We're going to go collect the other boxes, and you're going to give them to us."

"Lily, you don't want to do this," Laurel urged.

"How do you know what I want? I want my money! I want my kids back! I want my apartment back! I want my money!" Her eyes were wild, and Laurel knew she was beyond the point of reason.

Nevertheless, she still tried.

"I know Harold thinks I overheard your conversation, but I don't know anything, not really. As far as I'm concerned, this is a business deal between you and Mama G." Laurel took a tentative step forward, holding her palms upward so Lily could see them. She kept her voice soft and low. "I can help you, Lily, if you'll just let me. Don't force us to go with you. Because if you add kidnapping to your troubles, I won't be able to help."

"You can't help me, anyway." Her voice sounded weary and defeated, like yesterday in the ER. "I told you before. I'm past help. The best I can do now is get my money, and get Harold out of here. I'll send him away to live with my sister. It's the only way."

"No, Mama!" the boy said, a startled look filling his face. "You can't mean that."

"I do. It's the only way to save you."

"But I'm as guilty as you! I stole that car!"

"You stole it, but I drove it. Now hush, and open that door. Ladies, in the car."

Looking bereft, Harold did as he was told. Laurel's heart went out to the youth. She even felt sorry for his mother, despite what she had done. In her own strange way, Lily loved her children and was only doing what she thought was best.

As Harold opened the door and shoved Esmeralda inside, Lily barked, "The nurse sits up front, with me." She bent to look at the woman in the back seat. "I don't want to kill nobody again, but you know I'm capable. If you try anything smart, her blood will be on you." She straightened. "Harold, get in the car. You, too, Nurse Goody Two Shoes."

Cade took advantage of her distraction. When Lily opened the front car door and motioned Laurel inside, he picked up the trashcan and flung it aside. As it crashed to the ground ten feet away, Lily whirled around, giving him time to rush forward.

It also gave Laurel time to react. She shoved the car door back, knocking Lily off guard. Stepping out of the way, she shoved the lock down and slammed the door, locking Harold inside before he could respond. With the child locks engaged, the door wouldn't budge.

Lily staggered against the side of the car until she regained her footing. Looking dazed, she still managed to bring the gun back up, but it had a decided wobble.

"Don't even think about it!" Cade boomed.

He stood a few feet away, his long legs braced in a shooter's stance. Both arms extended, his gun was steady and unwavering as he leveled it directly at Lily's chest. With the light behind him and dressed in his cowboy attire, he looked like a larger-than-life hero from the big screen. Shadows hid his face, but Laurel had no doubt he wore a formidable expression. It was visible in his rigid stance. And she could hear the cold, hard threat in his voice.

"Lily, put the gun on the ground. Laurel, come here. Get behind me."

Not waiting to see if Lily obeyed, Laurel ran for the safety of his sheltering body. As she tucked in behind him, he hissed from the side of his mouth, "And this time, stay there!"

He then gave his full attention to the woman beside the car. "I mean it, Lily. Drop. The gun."

The wail of sirens flooded in from both sides of the street, as police cars converged on the parking lot. Looking helplessly around, knowing she was surrounded and outnumbered and at her wit's end, Lily dropped her gun on the ground and sagged against the car. Like a snowball melting in the sun, she sank to her knees and sobbed.

"Thank you," Laurel whispered, hugging Cade's stiff back. She buried her face into his shirt, refusing to think of what might have happened if he hadn't been there.

Instead of his sympathy, Laurel was on the receiving end of his wrath. His dark eyes snapped with anger as he turned just enough to stare down at her coldly. "What part," he ground out, "of 'stay put' don't you understand?"

It was close to midnight when Laurel opened her front door and stumbled inside.

"You didn't have to come inside," she told Cade as he followed her in. He had borrowed a cruiser to escort her home.

"Yes, I did." Without asking for permission, he pushed past her and went through each room, checking that all doors and windows were secure, and everything looked in order.

"There will be a patrol car making rounds tonight, just in case," he reminded her when he finished. He found her in the kitchen, making iced water.

"Would you like something to drink? Or something to eat?" It felt like it had been more than a mere five hours since they had eaten. It felt like a lifetime ago.

"I still have to go back to the station."

"This late?" she asked in surprise.

"Crime never sleeps. Neither do the people fighting it."

His manner was still so formal. Definitely back to the 'Nurse Benson' stage. Laurel sighed as she sank onto a barstool. "At least you're talking to me now."

It was still there, bubbling under the surface. His anger at her for having disobeyed instructions. "I wasn't sure it would do any good," he told her in a terse voice, "since you obviously can't listen!"

"I know, I know," she conceded. "I should have stayed at the table. I should have done as you said. But—"

"But nothing! You could have been killed tonight!" The very thought obviously brought him great angst. His brown eyes smoldered with lingering fear.

"But I wasn't," she pointed out needlessly. She dared to reach out and touch him. Beneath his long-sleeved shirt, his arm was as stiff and unyielding as steel. "I'm fine. Everything turned out fine."

A nerve worked along his jaw. "Is this the way it's always going to be?"

"What—What do you mean?"

His dark eyes bore into hers. "I don't know if a relationship will work between us, if you can't obey a simple order."

Laurel jerked her hand away and came off the stool, facing him with a defiant stance. "If you think you can bark out an order and have me obey like some little meek, timid mouse, then no, I don't believe it will!" she informed him.

"I'm not asking you to be a mouse. I'm asking you to be a level-headed, law-abiding citizen!" Cade flung back.

"You weren't on duty," she stubbornly pointed out, "when you told me to stay put."

"But I'm still a trained officer of the law! I knew what I was doing, and you didn't. You flagrantly put yourself in danger, when all you had to do was stay put like I asked, and wait for reinforcements to show up."

His glare was so intense, Laurel couldn't help but look away. "When you put it that way… And when you use the word 'flagrantly'…"

"This isn't a joking matter, Laurel," he snapped.

"I know. And I'm sorry." She pushed her hand through her dark curls. "I'm still a bundle of nerves, and exhausted, and right now I'm running on caffeine and adrenalin." She blew out a deep breath before peering up at him. "So, what happens now?"

"We'll throw the book at them. A dozen charges come to mind, for one or both women. Conspiracy to commit murder, intent to do bodily harm, intent to do bodily harm with a motor vehicle, theft of a vehicle, vehicular manslaughter, aggravated kidnapping, insurance abuse, insurance fraud… the list goes on."

"And Harold?"

"Because of his age, that's not as cut and dried. It will be up to the courts to decide whether or not to try him as an adult."

"I promised Lily I would try to help her."

Cade's sigh was heavy. "I know you did, but you shouldn't make promises you can't keep. She killed a man, Laurel. She deliberately hit him with a car, with the intention of ending his life."

"She was desperate," she whispered. "What about Icepick?"

"What about him?"

"He just gets away? That doesn't seem fair!"

"Nothing would please me more than to put that man behind bars, but we have nothing on him. Harold refuses to testify against him, still claiming that he tripped and fell yesterday. And that's the only charge that would possibly stick."

"What about extortion?"

"No proof. There's no law against loaning someone money and expecting a timely and profitable payback. At best, that's a matter for the IRS."

"So, he just walks free." It was a sad statement of the fact, not a question.

"For now, I'm afraid so. But sooner or later, we'll get him on something that will stick. I've got my eye on that man, especially now that he's threatened you. Believe me; he doesn't want to cross me." His look was like thunder.

Laurel hugged herself with trembling arms, thinking

of all that had taken place in the last week. She had seen her share of bad and evil things in the ER, but this hit close to home. In Houston, she could rationalize that it was a huge and diversified city, and that she was miles and lifestyles apart from the criminal element. But this was Bryan-College Station. A much smaller, more intimate community. The twin cities prided themselves on their hometown atmosphere and spirit of family. The seedy underworld wasn't supposed to thrive here. Wives weren't supposed to hire people to kill their husbands, and mothers weren't forced to do unspeakable deeds to provide for their families. It shouldn't be like that *anywhere*, least of all here.

"Are you going to be all right?" he asked, his eyes and his voice softening in concern. "I know you've been through quite an ordeal."

"Eventually," she said with honesty. "It may take a while."

He hesitated for a moment, before gathering her into his arms. "Come here."

Cade gave her a long, solid hug. She drew from his strength, feeling safe and protected for the first time since yesterday. As his arms encased her and cradled her against his chest, she felt the tension leave his body.

They clung to each other for a long time, until finally he pulled back and dropped his arms. "I should go."

She nodded, turning and walking with him to the door.

"By the way. That was good detective work tonight, Nancy," he admitted, a smile finally working its way across his tightly drawn face.

"Thanks. We make a pretty good detective team."

"Don't press your luck. I don't encourage armchair detectives, as you called yourself."

"*I* didn't call myself that. I was afraid *you* would call me that," she corrected.

"Do you have to argue with everything I say?"

"I was right about Mr. Miller, now wasn't I?" she said with a coy smirk.

At that, he actually laughed. Hearing the welcomed sound, some of the tension eased around Laurel's heart. Despite the hug, she was afraid she had damaged things between them beyond repair.

"Yes, you were." He paused when he reached the door. "Lock your doors," he said needlessly.

"Don't worry. I always do."

"Well, I guess I better head out."

"Cade?"

"Yeah?"

"Thank you for tonight. I can't even imagine…" She looked down at her fingers, nervously twisting them into a knot. She let that thought go, concentrating on another. "And earlier, when I asked what happens now… I, uh, I was talking about with us."

"Oh."

He hesitated for so long, she felt the color leak from her face. The hope leaked from her heart.

I blew it. The first guy I'm interested in since Kenton, and I blew it!

"Well," Cade said slowly, blowing out a breath. He took so long to continue, that she dared sneak a peek up at his face. Her heart tripped into overdrive when she saw the smile playing on his lips. "Not tonight. Not tomorrow night. Maybe not anytime this week. Maybe not even in the foreseeable future, judging from the workload on my desk." He made a weary grimace. "But one day, Nurse Benson, I'm going to take you on that dinner date we discussed."

Laurel rolled her eyes, but her lips curved in a smile. "Don't tell me we're back to Nurse Benson again!"

"No, Nancy," he told her, his dark eyes coming alight. "I think we've moved beyond that stage."

"I hope so," she admitted, the words coming out a bit breathless. *He has such gorgeous eyes!*

"I hope so, too. Because," Cade told her softly, moving in closer, "at night"—he touched her face and trailed long, gentle fingers over the graceful curve of her cheek—"when I lay down"—his voice was soft and low, as if he told her a deep, delicious secret—"I think," he continued, "of you"—his voice dropped to a mere whisper— "as Lovely Laurel."

He didn't kiss her. His eyes held hers in a caress, and she felt a connection to him through his touch. It was, in an odd way, more powerful than a mere meeting of their lips.

A slow smile spread across his handsome face, and he slowly moved away, turning to amble down her walk. The spurs were long gone, but his boot heels made a strong, promising keel against the stones.

"Don't forget!" Laurel called after him. There was a smile in her voice, even though he didn't turn to see it. "You still owe me those cookies, too!"

Author's Note

Not only is this the start of a new series, but it's also my attempt into an experimental cross-genre series. (I'm not even sure this is a thing, but I want to try it out.) *Cozy Cases of Mystery* will feature adventures with Laurel and Cade, while *Cozy Cases of Romance* will feature romantic stories involving the nurses and doctors of

Texas General. Stories on both sides will be clean, quick, and uplifting.

The only way I'll know if this works is if *you* tell me! Love the idea? Hate it? Please let me know what you think by dropping me an email at beckiwillis.ccp@gmail.com. This is book one in the mysteries, with book one of the romances, *A Hand-Me-Down Heart*, coming soon. Reserve your copy now.

I hate adding this part, but the best way to show your support and enthusiasm—and to help make the series a success—is to post a review on Amazon. Reviews on BookBub, Goodreads, Facebook, and word of mouth also have a huge impact on a book's success, so anything you do is much appreciated!

Thank you so much for reading.

ABOUT THE AUTHOR

Best-selling indie author Becki Willis loves crafting stories with believable characters in believable situations. Many of her stories stem from her own travels and from personal experiences. (No worries; she's never actually murdered anyone).

When she's not plotting danger and adventure for her imaginary friends, Becki enjoys reading, antiquing (aka junking), unraveling a good mystery (real or imagined), dark chocolate, and a good cup of coffee. A professed history geek, Becki often weaves pieces of the past into her novels. Family is a central theme in her stories and in her life. She and her husband enjoy traveling, but believe coming home to their Texas ranch is the best part of any trip.

Becki has won numerous awards, but the real compliments come from her readers. Drop in for an e-visit anytime at beckiwillis.ccp@gmail.com, or www.beckiwillis.com.